FIFTEEN MINUTES TO LIVE

FIFTEEN MINUTES TO LIVE

PHOEF SUTTON

The characters and events portrayed in this book are fictitious. Any similarity to real persons, living or dead, is coincidental and not intended by the author.

ISBN: 1941298761
ISBN 13: 9781941298763

Published by Brash Books, LLC
12120 State Line #253
Leawood, Kansas 66209

www.brash-books.com

"Well, I'd hardly finished the first verse," said the Hatter, when the Queen bawled out 'He's murdering the time! Off with his head!'"
"How dreadfully savage!" exclaimed Alice.
"And ever since that," the Hatter went on in a mournful tone, "he won't do a thing I ask! It's always six o'clock now."

For Dawn

WATER

She didn't know where the water had come from. It pulled at her and pushed her away. It dragged her down with its cold heaviness and forced its way into her mouth and all the time she fought it, she kept trying to figure out where it had come from and how it could be all around her under the night sky.

She had school tomorrow. She should be home. She should never be here, watching the stars bend and wrinkle behind the freezing weight of the salt water.

She pulled herself up to the air and tried to swim, but her arms ached as if she'd been swimming for hours. Perhaps she had. Perhaps she'd always been in this dark water. She thought about her little brother and her parents and how sad they were going to be. But her arms were tired and she wanted so much to rest.

She stopped and floated for a second. Then the wet got hold of her clothes and pulled them down. She watched the stars grow dimmer and more distorted through the water.

Then they came into focus again and she felt cold air on her face and a hard grip on her wrist. Wood scrapped her sides and something struck her face, but all she could see were the stars, which seemed impossibly bright now. She was too tired to answer when a voice asked if she was hurt. Too tired to care when she felt hands stripping her and searching her body. Too tired to answer the question, even if it had been asked in English.

"If she's not hurt, where did the blood come from?"

ONE

GLENDALE, 1994

Carl pulled into his driveway and the moon-cast shadow of the huge eucalyptus tree washed over the hood of his car and dappled the back of his hand that gripped the steering wheel.

He shut off the engine and in the silence of it dying, the music from the car stereo boomed much too loudly. Easing his head back against the leather headrest, he turned to look at his house.

Carl was the only person he knew who lived in the house he'd grown up in. He hadn't meant to. When he was seventeen he'd moved out of this cozy Spanish Revival house in Glendale (Glen-dull, all the young people called it) and over the hill to a grimy room over a store front on Hollywood Boulevard. No amount of pleading on the part of his parents, no amount of suffering of his own due to poverty or heart-break or the exciting starvation of youth could get him to move back in. In the end, it took financial security to do that.

Money had come into his life with the speed of a sudden head cold. One week he'd been scraping together enough money to Xerox programs for an abysmal production of his one-act plays in a converted toilet theater on Santa Monica Boulevard, and the next he was making two thousand dollars a week as a staff writer on a network TV show. Within two years he was a producer with an income approaching three hundred thousand a year. In the meantime, his parents' income had declined while the cost of living had gone up, so that the only money they had

1

left was tied up in their house. They didn't want to leave it, so they turned to him for help. The house he'd considered a sterile prison when he was a teen-ager looked like a worthwhile investment now that he'd hit thirty, so he bought it from them and let them live there for free.

A year later, just as he was recovering from the break up of his near-marriage, his mother died, so he moved into the house to keep his dad company. Now that Dad was gone too, there was no reason at all to stay there. He felt like an alien in the neighborhood filled with houses occupied either by elderly white couples or extended Armenian families of twelve.

So sell the house and buy a condo at the beach, he thought as he sat immobile in the driver's seat, Joan Armatrading blaring out of the CD player. It was two thirty in the morning. After a day like this, he should be rushing in to fall on the bed. Eight hours spent locked in a room with his partner, Kit, and four other professional manic-depressives, rewriting an ill-conceived episode of a new CBS half-hour comedy. That's three hours of writing and three hours of bitching about the actors and the network and how shitty all the other shows on television are and how the city is going to hell. And two hours of deciding what to order for dinner.

But he wasn't in bed. He was watching the blue-gray shadow of the tree move on the hood and thinking about all the times that eucalyptus shadow had washed over all the hoods of all the cars he'd known as they'd pulled into that driveway. The Chevrolet station wagon, while he was sitting on his mother's lap dribbling ice cream onto her slacks. His father's Dart when he was sixteen, driving home from a date with Jessica and smelling her scent on his fingers. His Maverick when he'd driven in from his Hollywood rat hole, deliberately too late for Thanksgiving dinner. His BMW when he'd rushed home after getting the call about his mother's stroke. Too late again, but not deliberately.

He started the car again and eased it forward, pulling up next to the kitchen door, leaving the eucalyptus shadow back on the trunk where he couldn't see it. He looked up at the darkened kitchen window and it was so empty it had made him catch his breath. He could already hear his footsteps echoing on the wood floors. He laughed to himself, entertaining the notion of reclining his seat and spending the night in his BMW. But somebody had to feed the animals.

He climbed out of the car. To hell with the real estate market, he really would put this house up for sale tomorrow. Some people have trouble keeping in touch with their pasts, he thought, I'm going to dump mine on the market at a cut rate.

———

He set the dish of dried cat food and an overripe avocado on the patio, slipped back through the double doors, settled into a wicker chair he'd pulled up for the purpose and waited.

His cat jumped clumsily on his lap. It climbed up his chest and breathed into his face, it's breath ripe with Science Diet for Older Cats. He pushed its head down, gently but firmly hoping it would curl up in his lap and go to sleep. Instead it climbed up onto his shoulder and started sucking on his hair.

This cat was an aged Persian. With old age, the flat face of the breed had turned positively convex, its teeth were exposed in a permanent werewolf's snarl and its snuggles of affection were accompanied by a viscous drooling. It was one of the most disgusting animals Carl had ever seen, but he kept scratching behind its ears. He even ignored the hair sucking, a life long habit he attributed to a premature separation from its mother's breast and, therefore, never had the heart to resent. He ignored the wet spot growing on his shoulder and peered out through the French doors at the bowl on the patio.

The raccoon showed up about five minutes later, scooping the dried cat food into his mouth by the handful. The cat jumped off Carl's lap and hissed at the intruder behind the protection of the patio door. Satisfied that it had done all it could do to protect its domain, it went off to the laundry room to vomit.

The raccoon paid no attention, moved on to the avocado and began to peel it deftly. All the while Carl kept perfectly still, amazed at the sight of the creature, as big as a small dog. Its haunches were huge and beautifully formed. He marveled at the ringed black tail and the black mask – like something out of a nature documentary right here in his own backyard.

For no reason that he could figure, it started suddenly and glanced up at him. Its black marble eyes met his and Carl tried to smile in a way that a raccoon might find friendly. It kept its eyes fixed on his as it ate the avocado.

He'd first started to suspect its presence about a week ago. He'd left a bowl of cat food out by the door over night by mistake and the next morning had found tiny hand like prints around the empty bowl. Since then he'd left out more food and found it gone every morning. Four nights ago he'd come in, late as usual, and switched on the light in time to see something that looked like a small bear waddling off into the dark.

So he'd spent the last few nights like this, sitting for a time in a chair in front of his patio window hoping to catch a glimpse of the beast. Now it was here, staring at him, apparently unimpressed, and Carl couldn't imagine how an animal of that size could live in an urban area. He knew that coyotes and even deer lived up in the hills, but he felt sure this fellow hadn't traveled that far. Somehow it had managed to eke out a living in suburbia. That was a miracle for any creature.

The animal dropped the bare avocado pit and trundled off into the darkness. Carl sat in his easy chair in the darkened room and watched it go. The encounter was over. The climax of ten days of careful planning had been reached. He had achieved contact with a fellow creature and had, in a small way, helped ease its struggle for survival. Their eyes had met and, on that basic level, they had bridged the gap that separates the species.

Carl was too depressed to get up so he fell asleep in the chair.

———

Carl woke up annoyed. He couldn't remember any details from his dream, but he had a vague image of himself rearranging the shelves in his garage, buck naked and surrounded by network executives. Nightmares he didn't mind so much, but what was the point of going to sleep if your dreams were only as annoying as real life?

It took him a few seconds to wonder what had woken him up. It might have been discomfort from sleeping in the chair, but his back didn't hurt. He couldn't hear the cat tromping around and screeching as she often did when he was just drifting off.

He heard a snapping sound and sat up fast. There's nothing as loud as a sudden sound in an empty house at night. He peered through the darkened window for any sign of the raccoon. There was nothing. He lapsed back to normal breathing.

The snap again. But it wasn't quite a snap now that he listened closely. It was a crack and a rattle and it came from upstairs. He turned toward the stairway, which seemed a long way off.

Crossing to the stairs was easy as long as he didn't hear the sound. When it cracked and rattled again he stopped dead, his heart pounding in his chest. Really pounding, he noted in surprise, picturing it bouncing off his ribs. And yet there was no sense in being afraid. There was nothing dangerous about the sound. He couldn't imagine a burglar up there, rifling through his drawers while dropping marbles, or whatever they were, at regular intervals.

In the silence he made it halfway up the stairs, two trains of thought fighting for his attention like overheard conversations at a party. One had his cat disinterestedly playing with a ping-pong ball; the other had the same ball played with it the same way by a bloodied serial killer. He laughed, then jerked still when the rattle came again.

This time he knew his fear wasn't physical. There wasn't anything up there that could hurt him. He was afraid because he recognized the sound but couldn't place it. He only knew that it came from a long time ago and that it didn't belong there now. It was a ghost sound. Like the laughter of phantom children and the bouncing of invisible toy balls in a Seventies made-for-TV horror film.

He ran the rest of the way up the stairs and into his study, the room that used to be his bedroom. The window overlooked the back yard and through it he could see the night sky, heavy with a thick haze that trapped the lights from the city and turned them back in a perpetual twilight. The light made it easy to see the handful of pebbles sailing up toward the window. The larger one struck the glass with a crack, the smaller ones rattled against the sill.

He stood in the doorway, blinking at the window in disbelief. He knew what it was now. Even if he hadn't seen it, he'd have known just from being in the room. The sound was different here, it was welcome, it was waited for, it was the sound he couldn't sleep for praying it would come. It was the sound that was as far from frightening as any he'd ever heard. Except that he hadn't heard it for seventeen years and it couldn't possibly be real.

His bed had been in the far corner. When he was seventeen he had lain awake in it every night in a sweat, wondering if that sound would come. If it didn't, he'd fall into fevered sleep in the early morning and twist through delirious dreams with a harem of women from all parts of the earth. If the sound did come he would creep from his bed, slip on his bathrobe and sneak down the stairs, his dick pivoting wildly in front of him, leading the way she used to say, like a divining rod seeking out her moisture.

He'd open the French doors in the living room with exquisite care and rush out back to find her. Jesse would be there by the Eugenia bushes. Carl would rush into her arms and they would kiss clumsily, not from lack of expertise, but because you couldn't kiss like they needed to and do it with any refinement. And any pretense of refinement was out of the question anyway, with his cock digging into her leg. That was part of the kiss as well, like his hand rubbing her pussy through her jeans. She would moan and he would tell her to be quiet and not wake his parents. "How would we explain what we were doing?" he would say laughing. And she would grab his cock and squeeze and say she thought this guy would explain things pretty clearly.

They would run into the greenhouse, stumbling, somehow holding on to each other all the way, and fall on the tarp and make love. His cock would be so hard he wouldn't even feel anything for the first few minutes, wouldn't even be sure he was in her unless he reached down and felt the join with his hand. Then sensation would come and they would climb all over each other and kiss and bite and who knows what, because in those days it didn't even matter what you did or even how long you did it because you were so overwhelmed by the sheer miracle of doing it.

Carl was so deep into his reverie; he half expected to see her standing in the back yard when he walked to the window. But that didn't stop him from being surprised when he did see her there.

She was standing below the window in a white summer dress, gesturing to him impatiently to come down. Or someone who looked like her was; it couldn't really be her. But it couldn't be anyone else either.

He opened the window and she spoke to him in a loud stage whisper. "Where the hell have you been?"

"Jesse?"

"Is something wrong?"

"Well..." But there wasn't, was there?

"Come on down."

He closed the window and crept out of the room, knowing full well he needn't worry about waking anyone. It didn't hurt to play act a little, and anyway it all had to be a dream. He much preferred this to the one about the garage.

As he descended the stairs he considered the possibility that this might all be real, feeling a wave of depression and apprehension. If it were real, it couldn't be what he'd been assuming – she wouldn't be there to re-enact a night of teen-age passion from the Seventies. The only thing that could make a normal woman sneak in darkness to the house of someone she hadn't spoken to in twelve years was some unusual and urgent kind of trouble.

He hesitated at the French doors, thinking for the first time in years of the circumstances of their parting and he was more sure than ever that no mere sexual whim would have brought her back here. He drew a deep breath as he opened the door and walked out into the night.

The raccoon had finished every bit of the dried cat food and spilled the dish of water all over the patio. He tracked the water out on the grass, trying to see her in the blue darkness. There was no one under the window, no sound of anyone around. If it was a dream, when had it ended?

An arm grabbed him around the chest; another reached between his legs and grabbed him there. He gasped and tried to pull away. Then he heard her laugh.

"It's me stupid."

She turned him around and kissed him. His mind was reeling from surprise to fear to pleasure, but it was soon calmed by a wave of memory. The thick, softness of her lips and the taste of cigarette on her tongue. Nothing like this could have brought her here, but her hand was running down his chest and into his jeans.

"What are you all dressed for? Did you think we were going on a hike?"

One of the first things he learned as a comedy writer was not to try to make a joke if he couldn't think of anything funny. So he just kissed her again and let her fumble with his belt. She backed away and touched his lip curiously, with her fingers.

"Since when did you grow a mustache?" she asked, sounding genuinely confused.

"I had to do something while I was waiting for you."

He kissed her neck and she giggled. "It tickles."

"You don't know the half of it," he murmured while nibbling on the tender flesh of her neck.

She gasped. It was a tender gasp, yearning and hungry, and at the sound of it Carl froze and felt his lips tremble on her neck. He knew that gasp so well, and it came from so long ago that he felt his heart grow in his chest. He shut his eyes and tears squeezed from them.

Jesse pulled away to look at him, puzzled. "What is it?"

He laughed. Only two tears had fallen. He was in control. He squeezed her arms, playfully. "It's just so good to see you."

"You silly."

In the old days she had always been the one to frighten him off with the depth of her feelings, now here she was, laughing at his emotion as if her showing up now were the most natural thing in the world. Didn't she know, or didn't she want to know, that he could stare at her in this darkness all night long? Was it all just a game to her?

She unfastened the top two buttons of his jeans and reached in. Any resentment he might have been feeling vanished in a surge of good will. "He's happy to see me too." There's an adorable tone of pride a teen-age girl gets in her voice when she realizes she can cause an erection. Grown women never have that tone, they know the potential for pain and confusion too well, or perhaps they're just bored with the whole thing. But a girl still thinks it's a marvel she can have that kind of power, and never thinks of what it might bring on. Jesse still had that tone in her voice. Carl thought his heart would break.

He pulled her close to him and kissed her again. She flinched for a moment when she felt the bristles of his mustache but he pulled her to him. He ran his hands over her body wildly, wanting to touch every inch, wanting to devour her. She pulled away again, laughing.

"Jesus, where have they been keeping you?"

He moved to her again, and they crawled over each other. It had been years since he'd gone wild on a woman like that, pawing and rubbing even though they were both still fully clothed. There weren't enough restrictions on adult sex to make it this exciting. He was pulling up her shirt and when she brushed him off, playfully. "Come on. Not here, your parents will hear."

He could have told her his parents were dead, but he didn't like to change the subject. So they ran to the greenhouse, clinging to each other just like the old days. Only they didn't feel like the old days. They felt like now. It was all the things that had happened since that seemed like distant memories.

"What happened to the avocado tree?" she asked as they passed the old stump.

"It died," he said, breathless.

"You're kidding?" She sounded genuinely shocked and he thought of telling her that time does pass and she couldn't expect all the things to remain the same and that was all a part of growing old gracefully and accepting the passage of the years, but he grabbed her tits instead. She laughed and dashed ahead into the greenhouse.

He was on her in a moment, swinging the door shut behind him and touching every part of her. He stripped every bit of clothing off her and himself, which was an insanely dangerous thing to do, considering his parents might burst in any second. And he couldn't help but consider that. He couldn't help but travel back, using her body as a time machine. He forgot that he'd ever been with another woman and fell back into the patterns of Jesse as if he'd made love to her yesterday, making circles with his fingers and tongue, pressing and pinching and biting in all the magic places. Hearing her gasp and cry out the magic sounds, seeing her white flesh turn ruddy as it blushed and her muscles tightened and her back arched and the sounds stopped, even her breath stopped as she pushed herself up at him and his mouth filled with her taste. Finally the sigh and the shudder came, she fell back to the earth floor of the greenhouse. Tears came again to him and this time he couldn't stop them. He rubbed his face against her and mingled his wetness with hers.

She twined her fingers in his hair and shushed him like a loving mother. Then she pulled him up onto her and it was a long time before they were still.

———————

When it was over she fell asleep. He realized that he'd never seen her sleep before. There was never that kind of time in the old days. She'd always rush out after a cigarette or two, each time professing to be shocked that she'd taken such chances.

He studied her face. The moon had made its way through the haze and was falling on her through the skylight. He was relieved to see that she did look older. This was no visit from the Twilight Zone after all. There were tiny wrinkles around her eyes, a smile line at the sides of her mouth, a very slight sagging of the flesh on her throat. Her body had changed too, a little broader below, but he liked that. There was a scar on the side of her belly, perhaps from an appendectomy. Its bright redness contrasted vividly with the paleness of her skin. He liked that too.

He nuzzled up to her and tried to pretend that she might like the added inches on his own gut. He felt as if it might be possible to ignore all these details and just close his eyes and go back to a time when they'd both been impossibly young. When they'd wanted each other so much they'd thought they were in love. But what if he did? The morning would still come, her game would be over and she'd be on her way. Don't pretend that makes you angry, he told himself. What the hell would you do if she wanted to stay?

He opened his eyes and was thirty, with a set of car keys digging into his back, laying on the hard dirt floor of a run down greenhouse, hugging a woman he hadn't seen or heard from in twelve years, wondering what she was doing here. Women are always complaining about men falling asleep after sex, but Carl preferred that to staying awake and thinking.

He shifted a bit, slipping the car keys to a less painful location. She awoke suddenly, gasping as if she didn't know where she was, then she nuzzled up to him, contented.

"I fell asleep," she apologized.

"I took it as a personal compliment."

"Silly. What time is it?"

He retrieved his watch from under the pile of clothes. "Four thirty," he told her.

"Shit!" She was up and scurrying around for her clothes. "Why the hell didn't you wake me up? Mom's gonna kill me."

"How _is_ your mom?"

"She's gonna kill me, that's how she is. Where the hell are my clothes?"

He gave her the white sundress and she looked at it, puzzled, as if she'd never seen it before. "What's that?"

"Your dress."

"Oh, yeah," she said doubtfully. She took it and started slipping it on. "God, I hope I can get home before she wakes up."

"I'll drive you."

"Oh right, you're going to wake your dad up and ask for the keys."

"I have my own car, Jesse."

"Since when?"

"I don't know, 1978?"

She looked at him in angry annoyance. "Stop being weird." She looked closer. "Where the hell'd you get that mustache?"

Carl was getting annoyed.

Jesse brushed by him and headed out into the yard. He followed her. She was heading for the gate, so he called out to her. "I told you I was driving you home."

"Keep quiet! Do you want to get us killed?"

He took her arm and led her to the patio and into the house. He flicked on the light and his eyes ached with the brightness. She snapped at him, "Carl, what about your folks?"

He turned and faced her. Just because she still lived with her mother, why should she think he did? Why should she think he still lived here at all? Unless some mutual friend had told her. But then she would have heard that his parents were dead. And no matter how much she wanted to play her stupid game, that was hardly something to joke about. "They're not here," he said, sharply.

"They're not here!" She seemed suddenly angry. "Then why the hell did you drag me out to that old greenhouse if your parents weren't here?"

"Isn't that what you wanted?"

"Why the hell would I want to lie down in the dirt when I could have a bed?"

He was getting sick of this. "Look what are you trying to do?"

"I'm trying to get home so I can get to class tomorrow."

"You're taking classes?"

"What the fuck are you talking about? Of course, I'm taking classes."

"Are you going to college?"

"I don't know. I haven't decided." She stopped suddenly and stared at his 70-inch projection TV. "Christ, that's a big TV. What are these things?" She was examining his home entertainment center.

"You know, CD, VCR, laser disc player."

But she wasn't listening; she was looking around the room in confusion. "Where'd you get all this furniture? Everything's different."

"Of course everything's different. What the hell did you think, everything was going to stay the same?"

"But..." The confusion on her face was undeniable. Carl decided to cut the crap.

"What are you trying to pull? Is this some game? If you want to fuck me once and never see me again, just tell me!"

She backed away from him, hurt and afraid. "You know how I feel about you."

"No, I don't. I don't know anything."

She shook her head, trying to brush it all away. "I don't like this, let's not do this. Just take me home."

He gathered up his keys and wallet from the mantelpiece. "Where do you live?"

She turned on him screaming, "You know where I live!" She was shaking with anger and frustration that was close to tears. He hurried to her in surprise and held her. Feeling her warm body sobbing against him, she was the little girl again and he was her boy. He'd been right when he first saw her, something was wrong. Why wouldn't she tell him what it was?

"I'm sorry," she whispered. "I hope your parents didn't hear."

"They're not here."

"What?"

"They're not here."

"Where are they?"

"They're dead, Jesse."

She pulled away from him, wiping her nose with the back of her hand. "That's not funny," she said as she headed out the front door.

They climbed into the car and she looked around her impressed.

"Where'd you get this thing?"

"I stole it," he told her.

They drove along in silence. Carl figured from her outburst that she lived in the same house, but that hardly made his question anything to get angry about. Nowadays people don't live in the same state they grew up in, much less the same house.

That, however, was the least of the mysteries of the evening. For the life of him, he couldn't figure out what she was up to. She lived at home. Perhaps she was divorced recently. Feeling unhappy with life. Wanting an evening of youth. But how would she have been so sure where he lived? Well, he thought with a laugh, she could have done something damnably clever like look him up in the phone book.

So she's sitting at home with her elderly mother, watching late night TV, feeling the urge. She looks him up in the phone book, sneaks to his house, (How? Did she really walk the mile to his house? Did she ride her bike, like she used to in the old days?) throws her pebbles and just assumes that he'll play along? It was crazy. But he did play along. And could he honestly say he was sorry he had?

So maybe he should stop complaining and enjoy what had happened for what it was. Maybe she was right. Maybe the only way for it all to work was to pretend that no time had passed.

"Is that Springsteen?" she asked.

He hadn't noticed, but "Better Days" was playing on the radio.

"Yeah."

"He sounds so different."

"Yeah, a lot of people think so."

"What album is this?"

"'Lucky Town.'"

"How did you get that one?" She was looking at him, puzzled. "Where'd you get that stupid mustache?"

"I grew it." When was she going to drop that?

"Oh, right," she said doubtfully. "It makes you look older." She looked at him more closely. "A lot older."

He had to drive up and down her street twice before he realized that her house wasn't there anymore. Somebody had torn it down and put up one of those white angular monstrosities that filled the lot with only inches to spare.

He pulled over and asked her, confused, "Is this it?" Then he looked over at her and saw the horror in her eyes. "Where's my house?" She asked, her voice small with fear. "There's the Rooney's house, there's the...Jesus, where the hell's my house? Where's my house?"

Carl reached out to hold her, but before he could reach her she was out of the car. He leapt out to follow her. She was pacing the dark street, staring at the impossible building in front of her.

"I know this is the right place. How could it be gone? I was just here. How could they take it away?" She was seized with a horrible new thought. "Mom and Dad...and Jeff, are they okay?"

She broke into a run, heading for the house. He grabbed her and she staggered to a stop. "I gotta get in there," she was trying to pull away. "I have to find out if they're in there."

"They're not in there," he told her.

"How do you know?" she asked, and suddenly he seemed as threatening to her as everything else. "Do you know something about this?"

"No, but it's obviously something very serious and you can't go off and do something that might be...dangerous. Right?"

She looked back at the house, warily. "Yeah," she agreed.

He took her back to the car as slowly and carefully as he could and sat her back in the front seat. "Now let's think about this. When did you see the house last?"

"What kind of question is that? This morning."

"And what did you do this morning?"

She was annoyed. "I don't know..." He could see her realize the truth of what she said. "I don't know. That's funny. I can't remember." She tried to shrug it off. "Just what I always do, got ready for school."

"What school?"

"What do you mean? Our school."

He took both her hands and moved close to her so he wouldn't have to ask the question too loudly. "Jesse, what year is it?"

"This is silly. It's 1976."

"And how old are you?"

"Seventeen. Are you okay?"

He took her in his arms and kissed her once before he turned on the car's interior light. "Look at me."

She looked at him in annoyance, but she kept looking. She looked for a long time.

"You don't look so good."

"I look older." He let go of her hand long enough to press the button that locked all the doors. "Honey, I'm thirty-five. It's 1994." She snatched her hands away. "Your house isn't there because somebody tore it down. I don't know where your parents are."

"Is this some stupid joke? I'm going home."

He pulled down the visor on the passenger side and slid open the mirror. She stared at her face in fascination. She seemed to trace each new line with her eyes. Then the full force of it hit her. She slammed the visor up and reached for the door. She couldn't open it; she couldn't even find the handle. She flung herself in a fury at the ceiling of the car. Carl tried to grab her, but she lashed out at him, smacking his nose and cracking his head against the window.

She tried to climb into the back and he grabbed her again, pinning her arms. She flailed about, slamming his knee into the steering wheel, gouging his shin with her heel. She kicked open the glove compartment and screamed a long wild howl before she began to cry.

He held her while she wept, feeling warm blood flowing from his nose, feeling the aching in his shin and the back of his head.

He'd had no idea she was that strong. She finally stopped crying and curled up next to the passenger door, silent, breathing heavily. He kept waiting for her to move, but she didn't. She was still. Maybe she'd passed out. He sighed and fell back on his seat, wiping the blood from his lip. He glanced over at her again, amazed at how peaceful she suddenly looked.

He drove back to his house. He couldn't think of where else to take her.

When they were there he touched her gently to wake her, not knowing what to expect. She stretched sleepily and looked at him fondly. "Did I fall asleep? I'm sorry."

He watched her closely. She didn't seem to have a care in the world. "Are you okay?"

"Sure I'm okay. Hey, what happened to you?"

He wiped the blood off his face.

She was concerned. "Did you get in a fight?"

"No. You're not upset?"

"About what?"

"About…about your house."

She shrugged. "My house is great." She looked at him more closely. "Where'd you get that stupid mustache?"

TWO

He watched her sleeping in his bed, her face blank and passive. A child with that expression looks like an angel; an adult just looks like death.

He'd convinced her that she'd gotten permission from her mom to spend the night at Julie Rafferty's, but that it was all really a plan so she could stay the night at his house since his parents were away. He was surprised how eagerly she took to this explanation, even though she didn't remember making any such plan. Any explanation, however weak, must have been worth grasping if it helped make sense of the horrible confusion that surrounded her.

She had no memory of what had happened when he tried to take her to the house. Once he'd gotten her into the bedroom, she'd wanted to make love again, forgetting all about their previous encounter and wanting to take advantage of the empty house. He'd had to beg off, pleading fatigue. She'd been hurt but he promised her the morning would be something special. Then she drifted off to sleep, peaceful and contented, not a bit concerned about her vanishing house and family.

What was he to do with her? She carried no I.D. with her, nothing to give him a clue as to her address. There was no listing for her in the phone book, or for her parents or brother. He'd noticed a white tan line on her ring finger, so she was married or divorced. She was in good health as near as he could see, clean and well taken care of. She obviously hadn't been wandering the streets. Unless this was some sort of temporary attack, he found it hard to believe she could function in the world on her own. People must be looking after her. But how was he supposed to find them? Put notices on telephone poles, like a child who's found a stray dog? The responsible thing to do would be to call the police.

He crawled into bed next to her and fell asleep.

———

She began to move restlessly next to him and he knew she'd wake up before long. He didn't think he'd slept at all, but he tried to convince himself he'd dozed off for a few minutes at least. Maybe she'd be better now. Maybe it was all the result of a drunken stupor and she'd wake up clear as a bell.

She sat up in shock. She looked around her in confusion, but seemed to feel better once she saw him.

"Carl? What am I doing here?"

He explained it all again, emphasizing that it was okay with her mom. He hoped against hope that she'd say, "My mom?" What the hell does my mom have to do with it? She's living in Florida and I've got five kids." But she didn't. She just nodded her head and said, "Oh, right," a little uncertain, but grateful all the same. Then she asked about his mustache.

He went down to make breakfast, keeping her with him all the time, keeping her talking to him, hoping that if she never broke her train of thought she might retain some information. It seemed to work for a while, until she interrupted the gossip about their twelfth grade history teacher to ask if she should set a place for his parents. Then she wanted to know about his stupid mustache.

While they were eating he tried an experiment. He took his car keys and put them in a drawer of the sideboard, telling her to please remember where they were since he was always losing them. She assured him she would, a little sarcastically. They talked. He waited exactly one minute, then asked where his keys were.

"How should I know?" she said, "They're your keys."

She didn't remember where they were, or even that she'd been asked to remember.

In the fifteen minutes it took them to eat breakfast he tried the same experiment five times, always with the same result. She didn't get tired of it. The last time he asked her to write him a note so he'd be sure to remember. She thought he was nuts, but she did it, probably thinking it was a set up to a gag.

He looked at the note. "Your keys are in the sideboard with the napkins, you idiot. Love, Jesse." They talked for a minute. He asked where his keys were and as usual got no help. Then he pretended to find the note in his pocket. He was puzzled. When did she write this?

She looked at it genuinely confused. Yes, she agreed it was her writing, but for the life of her she couldn't remember writing it. She must have done it last night, she decided. "What the hell were we drinking anyway?" she asked.

She finished breakfast. She had no trouble with that. She didn't stop every minute, wondering how the food got on her plate or how to eat it. Some things were automatic, he decided.

She spent the morning in a lawn chair in the backyard. He watched her from the living room. If he went out there she'd ask him where the avocado tree went for the fifth time and he was tired of telling her. He saw her try to read a book. She'd spend a long time on one page and then give up. Then she sat and watched the birds clustering around the feeders, in seeming contentment. After a bit she looked down and was surprised to find the book at her side. She picked it up and tried to read it. She'd spend a long time on one page and then give up.

She's lost, he thought. Set adrift in time. With every passing second she was building a new reality from the clues around her, only to have it washed away as the second passed.

He'd seen enough TV to know about amnesia. He remembered *Shenandoah* and *Coronet Blue*, with Robert Horton and Frank Converse searching for their forgotten identities through series that were always cancelled before they could be found.

This was different though. Jesse knew who she was, remembered every detail of her teen-age life as if it were yesterday, indeed believed it was yesterday, but everything since then seemed to have been erased.

Worse than that, she had clearly forgotten everything since they had met last night, had lost the ability to remember anything at all for more than a few minutes. He shuddered at the thought. This was a loss of memory in a total, literal, horrifying sense. It was as if she were trapped in a tiny pocket of time, lost in an eternal now. And does she even know that she's lost? Does she know what a huge piece of her is missing? How can she, when she forgets even that she is forgetting?

At least here she knows where she is, he thought. She knows my face, aged though it may be, and the house, even with new furniture. What happens to her when she's somewhere else, with someone she doesn't know, or didn't know eighteen years ago? How terrifying to every second find yourself dropped in the midst of strangers in a world you've never seen.

She looked up at him and smiled. "Carl, what happened to the avocado tree?"

"It died," he told her.

"All of a sudden?"

"It might have been sick for a while. Who knows with trees?"

Carl sat down in the lawn chair next to her.

"It's beautiful out here," she said. The yard smelled sweet and peaceful and you could barely hear the highway.

"Look at that," she said. Two hawks circled high over the hills to the North. They always came out this time of day, to soar and play games and occasionally drop as fast as a stone to earth in search of prey. Carl loved to watch them. They were part of his back yard family, along with the raccoon and the dove that just sat in the birdbath on hot days and the escaped canary that spent most of his time near the feeder. He liked to imagine that the hawks were sparring, wisecracking lovers – a feathered Nick and Nora Charles. Jesse was the only other person who'd ever noticed them.

"They're beautiful," she said.

"You ever think about what's going to happen?" she asked. "I mean, after school and everything."

I could tell you what will happen, he thought. I could tell you the future, but that would be too cruel. "I suppose we'll get along," he said.

"No, I mean, like are you thinking of going to college?"

"Yeah."

"And do you think we should go to the same college?"

He stood up and walked over to the fence, not answering, not saying a word.

"Hey," she said, "don't get scared. I'm just asking."

Carl walked back to her and took her hands. Should he answer as he wished he'd answered? As he'd answer now? What did it matter? He could answer with any lie in the world and she'd never remember what he said. "We could think about going to the same school," he said.

She looked at him a little puzzled, but happy and he wondered if he'd taken too long to answer and she'd forgotten she'd asked the question. He kissed her.

"Where'd you get the mustache?" she asked.

They made love again. All the time he wondered if he was being evil. He knew he was taking advantage, but he told himself it wasn't entirely selfish. When they made love she seemed so totally at ease, her 'now' seemed whole and complete. There were no anachronisms to give her frightening glimpses of all that she'd lost. There were just their bodies and if they looked slightly older, in the dark they felt the same. So, even if only for a few minutes, someone joined her back there in 1976.

Or was he making excuses? Was it just that sex, like eating, was a process that didn't need memory?

He watched her sleeping again. Eighteen years. Had she grown since he'd known her? She must have changed, become a woman. Was all that erased too? Was she a woman now, or a girl? He brushed the hair from her eyes and wondered if they should go to the same college.

THREE

In her dream she was deaf and blind and her world was nothing but scent. Night blooming jasmine by her window, hot asphalt from the street, cinnamon and syrup on French toast, the milky smell of her mother's rose water, acrid smoke from her father's cigarettes, the sweet flower of her baby brother's newly washed head, the musk of Carl from his sweater she kept hidden under her mattress, someone's cigar she should know but could not place, a pervasive aroma of mint and lemon, again, maddeningly allusive, and wafting through it all, like a hot wind, the salt water scent of blood.

———

"Maybe you think that doesn't give me a lot to go on." Kit wanted to be impressive, so Carl let him, "But just the name, you'd be surprised how much you can find out from just the name. For instance, nobody ever thinks of something as simple as checking the phone book."

Carl told him he'd checked the phone book.

"Yeah well, you would, you always take the fun out of everything. No luck?"

"Not listed," Carl said.

"How 'bout your high school alumni organization?"

"Didn't think of that."

"Thank God for small favors. I'll start there."

Kit stretched his lanky body across the sofa and pulled out a leather embossed notebook, one of his many affectations. Carl's eyes kept drifting to the new color of his partner's hair – Jean Harlow platinum blonde. Kit was a homosexual of the old school, far too flamboyant to be acceptable in today's politically charged gay community. Once or twice they'd even cast him in episodes of the show, playing a gay character, and their gay casting director had objected that Kit was too much of a stereotype. But he'd been through the wars, Kit maintained, and he'd earned the right to be a queen.

He was in great shape, thin and improbably tall, with only his oddly bulbous nose betraying the fact that he was ten years Carl's senior. They'd met at Paramount, when Carl was delivering sandwiches and Kit was running the research department. They shared no interests and couldn't have been more different temperamentally, so they decided they were ideally suited to be writing partners. For nine months, they worked after hours at Nickodell's, scribbling on legal pads in a booth in the corner. After eleven spec scripts they started getting work and they hadn't looked back since. They didn't resent each other half as much as most partners, though of course, each secretly knew the other was dragging him down.

It was Kit's expertise in the research department that had prompted Carl to call him now. Kit had always bragged that he could find the answer to any question within an hour. Carl had decided to put him to the test.

There really wasn't much to go on here. Jesse's dad had been in real estate, but Carl didn't know what firm. Her mother had been a grade school teacher. "Would they be retired now?" Kit asked. "How old were they?"

Carl shrugged. "You know how it is when you're a kid, grown ups are just old."

"How about the brother? Any ideas what line of work he might have gone into?"

"He was ten. He wanted to be a fireman." Carl thought about Jeff. Always tagging along, especially when Carl wanted Jesse to himself. But even as a teen-ager, when one dislikes children so intensely because one is afraid of being mistaken for one, Carl liked Jeff. The kid knew how to laugh at Carl's jokes. And he was such pals with his sister. Jesse didn't play with him out of an embarrassed sense of duty, but for the sheer fun of it. It looked like so much fun that Carl couldn't help but join in, relaxing his constant effort to appear world-weary in the exhilaration of a wild game of capture-the-flag.

Jeff would be twenty-eight now and Jesse wouldn't recognize him if she saw him. "She was real concerned about him last night," Carl said.

"Okay, I'll find them or him or whoever. You could do it yourself, but it'll be good for my ego. You going to work today?"

Carl checked his watch. It was nine-thirty, and he was due at the office by eleven. Ordinarily, Kit would be at his gym now and his skipping that ritual was a true testament to their well disguised affection for each other.

"I don't see how I can leave her alone," Carl answered.

Kit nodded. "I'll cover for you, I'll tell everybody you're drunk."

"Thanks."

Kit looked out the window, thoughtfully. "You're going to have to leave her alone eventually, you know."

"But this won't take long will it?"

"Naw," Kit said and his tone was so openly false it could hardly be called a lie. "But you know, the police could do it faster."

Carl shook his head. "I can't do that to her." Where would they put her? He couldn't bear to think of her in a county medical ward. She wouldn't know why she was there, and no matter how many times they explained it to her, she'd never remember. Every second she would spend there would be that first awful second of discovering she was imprisoned. "She'd be terrified. I can't put her through that. Not when there's no reason. Somebody has to be looking for her. Her husband, her parents. All we have to do is find them and take her home. Don't you think that's a much more human way to do it?"

Kit looked through the back window and watched her water the flowers. "She's beautiful," he said. He flipped his notebook shut and slipped it into the pocket of his polo pants. "Introduce me to her again. Tell her my name's Nicholas this time. I always liked that name."

Carl thought he ought to be offended by Kit's flippancy, but he understood it perfectly. There <u>was</u> something exhilarating about being able to start over from scratch with her at any given moment. "No need to worry about that bad first impression," Kit had said.

"Hi, Jessie," Kit said walking up to her, his hand extended. "I'm Carl's cousin Nick. Carl's told me all about you."

"Oh, hi." She was open and friendly and nothing about her suggested that the same man had been introduced to her as Carl's friend Kit, Carl's friend Jack, and Carl's younger uncle Tod, all in the last hour.

Kit said goodbye, hoped they'd meet again, and they headed off to the door.

"Carl," she called after him. There was a pitch of fear in her voice. "You're not going, are you?"

He laughed and reassured her that he was only walking his cousin to the door. She smiled then and kissed him. It was a warm loving kiss and Carl was embarrassed for Kit to see it. She released Carl and he walked Kit out to the door.

"She...thinks we're still in high school," Carl muttered to Kit by way of explanation.

Kit just smiled. "Now I know why you want to handle this personally," he said.

"That's a stupid thing to say." Carl was surprised by his own anger.

Kit held up his hand in insincere defense. "Sorry, bad joke." He opened the door and glanced back at Carl. "Oh, by the way, good idea to lose the mustache, takes years off you."

Carl automatically stroked the huge expanse of his bald upper lip. "Thanks."

Kit hesitated, still not walking out the door. "You guys were real close, huh?"

Carl shrugged. "Well, you're always serious when you're a teen-ager."

"I wasn't. Why'd you break up?"

Another shrug. "Just the usual. You grow apart. Who remembers?"

"If you don't, nobody does." Then he reached out and touched Carl's arm and Carl flinched instinctively. "Take care of yourself." Carl watched him go, wondering what that was all about. He turned to see Jesse behind him.

"Who was that?" she asked.

He told her it was just somebody selling something.

She looked around in annoyed confusion. "Did you guys move the phone? It's not on the table and I need to call Mom."

Carl's throat tightened. "Why?"

"Cause I want to talk to her."

"But you just did. You just talked to her about a half an hour ago."

"I did?"

"Sure. She said she was going to the mall and she'd be gone most of the day."

She sat down on the sofa. "Oh yeah, right." She looked around the room, trying to place things. "When did you get all this new furniture?"

"It was an anniversary present from Dad to Mom. Like it?" He was getting better at making the explanations shorter.

"I didn't even notice it." She shook her head, trying to clear it. "Carl, this probably sounds crazy, but I think I'm having trouble remembering things. Like, I honestly don't remember calling Mom, and I know I must have seen all this stuff before, but...Do you think maybe I smoked too much pot and fried my brain or something," she said with a laugh that didn't take the fear out of her voice.

"No, no, it happens to everybody." As if that was supposed to mean anything.

"I mean, this sounds stupid, but I don't even know if I have homework tonight, or what books I'm supposed to be reading, or if I have class tomorrow, or...oh God!"

She looked up at him, not even trying to hide her fear now, as if the great hunk of nothingness in her life was suddenly being revealed to her. Carl reached out and held her. He heard her whispering but the only word he could make out was 'remember.' Then she kissed him long and hard, with a desperation that had nothing to do with lust and everything to do with survival.

When she woke up he told her his parents were out of town at his Uncle Tod's funeral. She accepted the explanation with her usual complacent gratitude. There was no sign of her earlier desperation. Such self-awareness was evidently rare – for her sake, Carl hoped it was very rare.

The doorbell rang and he threw on his bathrobe and ran down to answer it. Kit was on the doorstep, looking oddly child-like in the dusk. Carl asked if he'd found anything out about her.

"Yeah." Kit's voice was hesitant and uncertain.

"What did you find out?"

It took him a moment to answer.

"She's dead."

FOUR

S he had loved to sail, a preoccupation Carl had always found annoying. Southern Californians were, by birthright, obliged to love the ocean and the beach, but Carl was uncomfortable there. Hot sun tightened and pricked at his skin, lying in it made as much sense to him as voluntarily relaxing in a swarm of mosquitoes. Sand was useful as a tool for planing wood; letting it actually touch one's skin and collect in sensitive crevices as a form of recreation seemed contrary to the most rudimentary concepts of proper hygiene. And sailing, combining all these irritations with hard physical labor and rope burns, was a trial Carl found hard to endure.

But Jesse loved it and for her sake, and for the sight of her in a skimpy two-piece bathing suit, he had been willing to put up with it. And she was beautiful on a boat. Not because of the swimming suit, after all he'd seen her naked and nothing could compete with the wonder of that. The beauty came from all the clichés of the sea. The wind in her hair, the sunlight reflected in her eyes, the sweat glistening on her body smelling of cedar and milk. At times he caught sight of her on the deck and he was filled with a love for her that he could not understand. It had nothing to do with lust or friendship and it made him feel unspeakably sad because he was too stupid to know what to do with this feeling. He would know when he was older, he had told himself. He was older and had not felt it since.

So it was worth the sunburn and the bloodied palms and the pulled muscles and the constant refrain of her father snapping

"Not that rope," at him whenever he was given a task, and her little brother laughing joyously at all his mistakes, just to see her in her glory. She was a sea creature then, and he was a poor landlocked mammal condemned to strain for glimpses of her through the surf.

She'd drowned three months ago.

She'd gone sailing with her husband (*husband*, Carl squirmed when Kit used the word) and brother-in-law and had fallen overboard in a sudden gale. The husband had searched desperately for days with the help of the Coast Guard, but it was no use. The search was called off. The body was never recovered.

Carl and Kit looked at the body sleeping peacefully in Carl's bed.

"She doesn't look like a ghost," Carl said, after they had returned quietly to the living room.

"Have you ever seen one?" Kit asked, opening a bottled water.

"No."

"Then how do you know?"

"She's not a ghost, Kit."

"How do you know?"

"Because I'm not an idiot."

Kit shrugged and took a long swig from the bottle. "So what happened?"

"Obviously she made it to shore somehow. Someone rescued her. The accident must have injured her brain in some way so that she can't recall what happened. Or anything else."

"Okay," said Kit, in the same studied, critical tone he used when they were coming up with stories for their show, "where has she been for the last three months?"

"I don't know."

"When you found her, was she filthy, dirty, did she reek of the streets?"

"No."

"So someone's been taking care of her."

"Yes."

"But not telling her husband or the authorities?"

"Maybe they didn't know who she was."

Kit considered that, silently.

"Tell me about the husband," Carl said, uncomfortably.

"He's an investment banker, pretty well off. Lives in San Marino. His name is Martin Ackerman."

Carl picked up the phone book and started leafing through it.

"What are you doing?" Kit asked.

"Well, we have to let him know."

"Over the phone?" Kit looked dubious. "It's going to be a shock, don't you think?"

"Well, I don't know if I can break it to him gradually. I could start by telling him 'your wife's a little less dead than you thought,' and then work up from there."

"Well, you can't just blurt it out. There ought to be something you can do to prepare him."

Carl sat down on the couch, deflated by the thought of it. How do you prepare someone for a resurrection?

FIVE

It didn't look like her house.

A low-slung ranch house, all roof and hedges, hiding its face from the world, it had no trace of her openness, no sign of her welcoming smile. Well, maybe she'd changed since he'd known her. Then he thought of her waiting around the corner in the car with Kit and knew she hadn't changed at all.

They'd decided Carl should go in first and try to pave the way, so Kit had insisted they keep the car out of sight, just in case Ackerman might glance out his front window and see his dead wife in the back seat of a BMW.

He rang the bell, hoping a maid would answer so he'd have a few more seconds to figure out what he was going to say. A tall man in his forties opened the door. He wasn't the maid.

"Hello, are you Martin Ackerman?" Carl asked.

He nodded. Carl realized he'd have to come up with another sentence.

"I'm an old friend of your wife's. I was very shocked to hear about her death." That much was true. "Could we talk for a second?"

Ackerman looked at his visitor. Carl tried to figure out if it was sorrow or resentment or just boredom that lay behind his eyes. He nodded again and moved to let Carl pass.

There was no trace of her inside the house, either. It was a man's space, with heavy dark upholstered furniture and dark green fabric on the walls. Leaded windows diffused what little light could slip past the shrubs and roof. It was a room that guaranteed security from skin cancer.

What illumination there was came from three standing lamps, covered with thick shades. Carl made it to a chair without stubbing his toe and considered this a small victory. He tried to tell from Ackerman's expression whether he was expected to sit or not, but either it was too dim to make out or Ackerman had no expression. Carl sat down anyway.

"Somethin' to drink?"

Carl turned in surprise to see a maid next to him. She was in her late thirties, adorable, Hispanic, and almost completely round. He exchanged a few words with her in his hard won Spanish that always seemed to amuse native speakers so much. She laughed and went to get the coffee, leaving Carl alone with the problem at hand.

"Of course," Carl said, hating the way he started. "I hadn't seen your wife for many years, and then the other night..." the other night what? He backed off, tried another tack. "The other night I heard she'd died and, well like I said, it came as a great shock."

Ackerman agreed that it was a great shock.

Carl agreed with his agreement.

"You didn't tell me your name," Ackerman said. His voice betrayed no trace of interest. His face, topped by prematurely gray hair, showed no emotion. Was this the numbness of grief or a businessman's poker face?

Carl told him his name. Ackerman looked at him with a hint of surprise. "You knew her in high school, didn't you? Jessica... mentioned you."

Carl nodded, his face flushed with heat as he wondered what she might have said. "It was a long time ago."

"Yes," he said. "Then you know Jeffrey?"

"I did."

Ackerman took a letter from a desk by the window and handed it to Carl. "This came today."

Carl looked at the envelope. The postmark was Peruvian. He opened the letter and skimmed it. Jeff was working there with a Catholic relief fund. Carl remembered Kit's question about what Jeff might be doing now – he could have guessed for a long time and never come up with this. The note was filled with misspellings and bad grammar – evidently Jeff's scholastic skills had not improved.

To call it a letter was an exaggeration. It was a note, undated and written in haste to inform Jesse and Martin that someone named Father Vincent needed help in the interior and Jeffrey had volunteered. Since the countryside was "a little less developed than here in Ayacucho" (Carl shuddered at the thought) he was going to be "sort of out of touch for a while. Can't say how long really." "Jesse," he went on, "I know things are rough. Hope they aren't really as bad as Martin seems to think, but remember that the Lord is there for you. I know your rolling your eyes at that one, but you must believe it. I pray for you. Love, Jeffrey."

Carl checked the postmark before handing it back to Ackerman. It was dated two weeks ago. Two weeks after Jesse's 'death.' "He doesn't know?" Carl asked.

Ackerman slipped the letter back in its drawer. "We've tried to get in touch with him, but it's not easy. Perhaps he'll be happier for awhile, not knowing." His tone was flat and seemed to require no reply.

The maid, who Ackerman now identified as Mari, was with them again now, pouring the coffee in a happy bustling way, as if the room were sunny and filled with children. Carl wondered aloud if the American Embassy might be able to help locate Jeff and was surprised by her bitter laugh. Lima was her home, she told him, and she implied that Americans weren't the best people to go to for help there.

She bustled out the door and Carl and the room returned to its somber darkness. The wrong person owns this house, Carl thought. Give Mari a place like this and she could make something out of it. Jesse would hate this room, Carl thought, and he knew that that was the reason he wasn't telling Ackerman about his wife out in the car. But keeping the truth back wasn't an option, he reminded himself.

"It's a shame," Carl said, "that they didn't get a chance to see each other before…"

"Oh, they saw each other. Or at least he saw her."

Carl looked up surprised.

"Excuse me, but how much do you know about my wife's death?"

The abruptness of the question startled him. It was as if this were the first time Ackerman had actually spoken to him. "Almost nothing. I guess that's why I'm here. I hope I'm not intruding."

"Of course not. It must be very painful knowing you'll never be able to make your peace with her."

Carl looked away. She must have told him then, he thought, feeling himself blush. He took a sip of coffee to cover embarrassment and scalded his tongue.

"Her death was a terrible tragedy, of course, but in a way it might have been something of, well, a kindness." Ackerman took a breath, looking like someone who had told a story once too often. "She'd been very sick. Not physically…Well, no, it <u>was</u> physical, but…you see, I still don't quite understand it. She began to behave strangely. To forget things. We didn't take it seriously at first. It seemed like simple absent-mindedness. But then, one day we went shopping and I saw her pick out a scarf, then she came back and took another one, and another one. All the same scarf. I asked her why she wanted so many, and she didn't know what I was talking about, didn't remember taking even the first one. When I showed them all to her, she became hysterical. Things fell apart so fast after that. At first she'd have her bad times, but then she'd be fine again and we'd be so relieved, but then...In the end, her short-term memory completely disappeared. Do you know what that means? She couldn't remember anything for more than fifteen minutes at a time."

"We thought it was premature senility, Alzheimer's disease, we just didn't know. The doctors wanted to run tests, even though there were no cures for any of the things it might have been. I suppose they just wanted to be able to put a label on it."

"They were certainly impressed with what they found. It's not fair to say that they were pleased, but you couldn't deny that they were at least exhilarated to be working with something a bit off the beaten track. It's called Korsakov's Syndrome. It destroys the part of the brain that remembers."

"At first she just couldn't learn anything new. Then it started on her old memories, wiping them out, eating up more and more of her life. She forgot she lived in this house, wondered why we weren't at our old place in Pasadena."

"Then she forgot me. One morning she looked at me and I knew she hadn't the vaguest idea who I was. All our friends, the nurses, my family, they were all strangers to her. She was frightened of us, thought we were holding her prisoner. Wanted us to call her parents – she forgot they were dead."

"By the time she died, half her life was gone. She thought she was still a child living at home. Jeff came out here a week before she died. I thought he might be able to get through to her somehow, or at least be a familiar face for her. But she didn't know who he was. Her brother was ten years old and this was a man. He only looked familiar enough to frighten her."

"There's no cure?" Carl asked.

"No, no, the damage is irreversible. The doctor tried to comfort me, he said memory isn't all there is to life, he said I could still make her comfortable and happy. I can't think of what he meant. Unless he meant comfortable like a dog or cat and I couldn't think of her as a house pet. Can I get you anything? You look pale."

Carl tried to shrug him off.

"I'm fine. It just must have been very painful for you."

"Oh yes," he agreed, quickly. "It's horrible to say, but her death was a comfort to me. If I had to think of her living for another thirty or forty years among strangers who won't let her call her mother...Well, as I said, it may have been a kindness." He smiled a quick smile and started for the door. "I hope I was some help."

"Jeff...in his letter didn't seem aware of how bad off she was, but if he'd seen her..."

"Jeff is one of those people who believe that if you ignore a problem, it will go away. Only he uses the word 'pray' in place of ignore."

Carl tried to laugh. "I don't know if relief work in Peru is ignoring problems."

"Well, that depends on which problems he's ignoring, doesn't it?"

Ackerman opened the door. He was clearly being dismissed. Now was the time to tell him.

"But what happened on the boat? How did she die?"

Ackerman didn't want to keep talking, but he did. "It was the day after Jeffrey left. My brother Frank and Jessica were very close. They used to go sailing together, she always loved it. So he thought it might make her 'happy and comfortable,'" he spit the words, derisively, "to go for a sail. He was wrong. She forgot she'd ever known how to sail. She was terrified. We were caught in a squall, she became disoriented and panicked. Neither of us saw her go over, but when we looked around she was gone. We tried to find her. We couldn't."

There was no grief in his voice, just weary discomfort. Perhaps he'd lost his energy to mourn.

Carl had to speak now. "Look, I don't know how to say this, so I'm just going to...It didn't happen like that."

Carl meant to go on, he meant to say that she hadn't drowned, that someone had picked her up or she'd somehow made it to shore. But there was a startled look and then a stillness in Ackerman's eyes that made him stop.

"What?" Ackerman asked.

"After she was in the water. She didn't just go down like that..."

Even then Carl was going to go on, to stop this clumsy hemming and hawing and spit it out. But Ackerman stood and walked to the door and very quietly shut them in.

"How do you know that?" he whispered when he turned back. His look sent a cold chill through Carl and he knew they were talking about two different things.

"I know," Carl said.

He circled the couch, keeping his eyes locked to Carl's as he moved. "You were on the other boat?" Carl didn't shake his head. He didn't nod. He didn't do anything but try his best not to faint. Ackerman laughed. "You don't know anything. Get out of here."

Carl spoke without thinking. "I know she didn't drown like you said."

He regarded Carl in silence for a moment. "Well, you're certainly living up to her descriptions of you." Carl didn't even blush at that. He just kept focused on Ackerman, the way a dancer focuses on a spot when twirling, to keep from kneeling over. Ackerman pulled a checkbook from a table by the window. "What do you want? Money?"

Carl didn't answer.

"Come on. I know you're making it all up, but I don't want you causing trouble. How much do you want? I'm in a giving mood."

Carl weighed his answer. "Twenty thousand."

Ackerman laughed and threw the checkbook back in its drawer. "Get out of here."

"I know someone who saw everything that happened on that boat," Carl said, and he wasn't even lying.

Ackerman stared at him for a long while, then he took the checkbook out, scribbled on it, tore out the check and handed it to Carl. It was made out to cash for twenty thousand dollars. "Get the hell out of here."

Carl's hand was shaking as he took the check and walked slowly out of the room. He passed Mari but never focused on her. He was surprised he could make it to the door. His hand was cold with sweat when he turned the doorknob. Ackerman stopped him then, with a whisper.

"Don't come looking for more."

Carl nodded and was out the door in the bright sunshine, blinding after the darkness of that room. He crossed the lawn, stumbled on the curb, feeling Ackerman's eyes on his back, clutching the wet check in his hand.

He rounded the corner, walking into the hissing sprinklers of a corner house, the coldness of the water hitting him with a shock. He fell to his knees and spit. He tore the check to pieces and threw them down the sewer. He sat on the green lawn and let the fake rain fall on him as he played the conversation back in his mind.

He took a deep breath and struggled to his feet. Time to get back to the car and make sense of all of this. Tell it to Kit and to Jesse and see if he could figure out what to do next.

He took one step and stopped. Kit was standing in the spot where the car was supposed to be, looking around him in confusion. Carl hurried to him. "Where is she?" he asked.

Kit looked at him apologetically. "She left," he said.

SIX

Her locker wouldn't open. She tried the combination six times and it still jammed on her. Typical. She smacked it with her fist. Typical. Ten minutes late to Delgado's class and she can't even get her book. He'd flay her alive if she came in like this.

She walked down the empty hallway, listening to the rumblings of classes in progress and cursing under her breath. She could try going to the library, see if she could check the book out, try to fake it. But now she didn't even remember what chapter they were on. Come to think of it, she couldn't quite remember the name of the book. Delgado would love that.

The best thing would be to cut her losses, skip class and wait till fifth period. Tomorrow she could tell Delgado she couldn't come because she was having real bad cramps. Delgado got so embarrassed whenever a girl talked about her body that he'd gladly believe her, just to shut her up.

"May I help you?" The voice rang out to her down the hall.

She turned and saw the teacher. No one she knew, thank God. She ducked down the next hallway and ran to the auditorium. She slipped through the side door and ran down the dark aisle, her footsteps echoing in the empty theater. This was always the safe place, the haven. No one but the drama students ever came here, except during the assemblies. The dark emptiness scared them off.

She clambered up the foot of the stage and ran past a ratty, old rehearsal sofa center stage (what dump did they drag that out of?, she wondered), past the 'ghost light' on its wooden stand (old theater superstition, she remembered, keep that light burning at all times, so the ghosts can see) and on into the soft, black curtains of the wings. She kept running though she knew no one was following her, just enjoying the feeling of running. There was a wire cage off stage left that held the lighting equipment – ancient electronics controlled by huge wooden levers, like something from Dr. Frankenstein's laboratory. Set into the wall, next to the refrigerator sized gray metal boxes filled with fuses and tubes, there was a trap door.

She slipped off the always-unfastened padlock and opened the door to the cage. She squeezed between the dimmer board and the metal shelf with its rack of lighting gels, crouched down, opened the trap door and crawled into the even darker blackness within.

They called this the Black Hole of Calcutta. She thought Calcutta was somewhere in India, but didn't know why it had a black hole. This Black Hole was a crawlspace inside the walls of the auditorium. There was a metal ladder bolted to the cinderblock walls, which rose thirty feet to the ceiling of the theater. If you climbed it and walked along the ridiculously unsafe catwalks, you could adjust the lights that beamed down on the stage. It was either unknown or deliberately ignored by the school administration that students regularly clambered like monkeys thirty feet above hard wooden seats and linoleum, risking death and devastatingly high insurance premiums with every step.

The students themselves would have been the last people to tell anyone about it. They loved the risks of the high wire act. More than that, they loved their secret cave, which they used for much more than theatrical lighting.

She breathed heavily, enjoying the drama of the chase, even though she doubted that the strange teacher had even taken two steps to follow her. She started climbing the ladder, feeling, as always, like an old time sailor climbing a mast on a stormy night.

She made it to the top, tired and surprisingly out of breath. Was she getting out of shape? She lay on the catwalk, inhaling dust, looking into the darkness above her, watching it grow brighter as her eyes collected the light drifting up from below. She rolled over onto her stomach and looked down – the ceiling was below her now, or the asbestos panels that made up the ceiling as you saw it from the floor. She stood up, wondering why her legs ached so much, and walked to the lights. They hung from a metal bar suspended from the concrete, their lenses pointing through a long slit in the ceiling. Looking over the lights she could see the stage below, in the faint 60-watt glow of the ghost light. She loved watching the world from up here. Everything seemed so much more interesting from a distance.

It was weird, though, that she didn't see anyone down there. And why didn't they turn the lights on? What was the point in sending her up here to adjust the lights if they weren't going to turn them on and tell her where to point them?

She called down to the stage, but no one answered. And now that she thought about it, she couldn't actually remember them sending her up here. So why was she here? To meet Carl? Weird that she couldn't remember.

She settled down to think it over.

———

All through the endless forty-minute cab trip to Glendale, Carl hadn't spoken a word to Kit. He just listened as Kit switched from heartfelt apology, to defensiveness, to outraged accusation.

"You're telling me you handled this in the best possible way, that this isn't your fault, you telling me that?"

Carl wasn't telling him anything.

"What took you so long? You were just supposed to prepare him a little bit and then take her to him, you weren't supposed to leave me out there with her that long. You can handle her, I can't."

She gives me the creeps. She kept forgetting who I was; you knew she'd do that. What the hell were you gabbing about?"

Carl wasn't gabbing now.

"Why didn't you tell him?"

Carl didn't say.

"Two minutes I was gone. Less than that," Kit repeated.

He told Carl again how he'd waited so long and been so nervous that he'd had to pee, so he just slipped out of the car ("okay, I didn't time myself, but I was there and I was back and how long can it take to piss?") to some bushes behind a house under construction. When he got back ("I'm serious, ten seconds, tops, fuck you if you don't believe it") the car was gone and Carl was staring at him angrily.

"How was I supposed to know she'd steal the fucking car? Where the hell are we going? Why don't we just call the cops? I think you've already fucked this up enough on your own, if you don't mind my saying, and I know it hurts, but I'm just saying what I believe to be true."

"I don't think the police are such a good idea," Carl said. He knew where she would have gone. She would have tried to go home.

But Carl's BMW wasn't in front of the big white house when they climbed out of the cab. Maybe they'd beaten her there, Carl thought, trying to keep his heart from sinking. If she wasn't here, if she'd really fallen through the cracks and was out in the world on her own, how would he ever find her?

He rang the front bell and the little window in the door was opened with more than customary caution.

Carl described Jesse to the frightened woman. He didn't have to ask if she'd been there.

"What's wrong with her?" the woman asked, eyes wide. "I mean I'm not paranoid, I try to be as helpful as the next person, but this is getting scary. She comes here asking about people I've never heard of, saying she knows they're here and what have I done with her house. How can a person do something with a house? I just had to slam the door on her; I just had to bolt it. Then she starts hammering on the door. I mean hammering, really hammering. And yelling. Finally she just drove off...No, she didn't say, and I really don't care where she was going. I just want some assurance, if you know this woman, I want some assurance that she won't come back again. These days you have to wonder, you can't help it, you have to wonder if you're safe. And I'm not paranoid, but I don't want to think some psychotic has focused on my house and is going to do something, I don't know what."

Carl told her not to worry. That she was sick, but that she'd never hurt anyone. "I hope you're right," she said, "but I can't say I believe you. She gets worse every time."

Carl had turned to leave but he stopped now. "She was here before?"

"Yeah, last night. It was very late. It must have been nine o'clock. But I said to myself, she seems confused then and I thought well, maybe it's an honest mistake. And I figured I was making more out of it than I should, because I was tired and who doesn't get a little paranoid when they're tired? And I'm not paranoid."

"How did she get here? Did she have a car?"

"Yes, some black sedan, I didn't really notice," she said, suddenly sounding suspicious.

Carl thanked her and promised Jesse wouldn't be back, though he knew he only said that to have an exit line. He didn't see any reason she wouldn't be back there every five minutes.

Kit was still sulking in the cab, didn't even ask Carl what the lady had said. Carl ran it over in his head. She'd come by here last night too, before she'd come to his house. That made sense. Somehow she'd gotten hold of a car, probably in a manner similar to the way she'd gotten hold of his. Someone was driving her somewhere, had left her alone long enough for her to drive off, either in a deliberate escape or because she forgot about him. Then she'd driven long enough to forget about all that. So she'd find herself driving a strange car, but naturally she'd drive it home. And even if she forgot where she was at every stoplight, she'd still know to go home. So she'd come home and found home gone. Then hours later she'd showed up at his house. Where did she go in between times? Wherever it was, that was where she'd go now.

So he could just go home and wait, assuming that the pattern would repeat itself and that eventually she'd show up at his door. But could he really be that cool? Could he really just sit and wait, hoping that nothing would happen to her between now and then?

He told the cabbie to take them to his house and thought about that black sedan. Then he remembered something – those car keys digging into his back in the greenhouse. They hadn't been his.

Until then he'd never really stopped to consider how she'd gotten to his house. He remembered no black sedan parked anywhere nearby. So she'd left it somewhere, but kept the keys. And that somewhere was the place she went between her house and his and, chances were, that was where she was now.

———

"Fuckinkids." To Manny, the custodian of Fremont High School, this was one word, and the only word to describe the student body of Fremont High School. There were ten days when it was the only word Manny used at all.

Friday was his hardest day. Cleaning up the shit and garbage the fuckinkids spread all over the school all week. Like it mattered. Like the fuckinkids wouldn't do it all over again next week. And he'd clean it up. And the fuckinkids would do it again. And again. And again. Manny felt that made little contribution to society.

And the fuckinkids laughed behind his back, he knew that. Half the filth they left, no <u>more than half</u>, was just for his benefit, just so he'd have to clean up after them, while they laughed at him.

And now the trapdoor behind the stage was open again. The fuckinkids were getting up there again, doing their shit so he'd have to clean it up. Well, he wasn't going up there. He wasn't climbing the fuckinladder to sweep up their beer cans and joints and used rubbers and their shit. Once they'd actually done that, the fuckinkids had actually shit up there, through the ceiling, trying to hit the principal during an orientation address. And everybody went ape shit, saying how could they treat the principal like that. But Manny knew it wasn't the principal they were after. The principal didn't have to clean it up.

Manny slammed the trap door shut and fastened the padlock in place. Monday he'd nail the fuckinthing shut for good. Before he moved off, he wondered if someone might be up there now. Serve 'em right. Leave them in there over the weekend. Give 'em time to think. Let 'em know Manny could fight back.

Fuckinkids.

———◆———

Carl lifted the keys from the dirt behind a broken flowerpot. Thick flat keys, with a heavy black plastic base. The Mercedes symbol was a button, when you pressed it, you could lock or unlock the doors from ten feet away. But you had to have some idea where the car was to be ten feet away from it.

Carl sat on the dirt floor of the greenhouse, leaning back on the old wood and peeling paint, staring at the spot on the ground where the dirt was swirled and swept about from their loving embrace last night and eighteen years ago.

SEVEN

"I'm just asking you to consider the possibility." Kit sounded so matter of fact, Carl wanted to scream.

"Why? It's inane, it's idiotic."

"But you can't find her, can you? She's disappeared, hasn't she? Just like she was never..."

"Don't finish that sentence. Please don't finish that sentence. She stole my car, for Christ's sake. Do ghosts need cars?"

"How can we be sure what they need?"

Carl stood up and frightened half a dozen finches from the feeder. "This isn't helping."

Kit remained irritatingly calm. "Why don't you go to the police, if you're so sure of your theory?"

"You mean my crazy theory that she's a real person? They might put me away."

"Don't evade the question."

Carl sat back down. "The police would just give her back to him."

"And you're sure that would be bad?"

"I'm not sure."

"Well, then."

"It's just that he said I was making it all up."

"Maybe he thought you were."

"But I hadn't said anything yet. What did he think I was making up? I hadn't even said anything and he gave me money. Twenty thousand. He had to be feeling guilty about something."

"Maybe he just feels guilty about the accident. A lot of people in this world feel unjustified guilt."

"Yeah, but it's pretty justified if you've just killed somebody."

"You think that's what he did?"

Carl took a deep breath and took the plunge. "I think he figured a quick shove off the end of the boat was easier than spending the rest of his life with…"

"Mercy killing?"

"So that makes it okay?"

"It makes it understandable."

"You know, that's your fucking problem, you understand everything."

"Thank you."

"Look, it's not like she's dying of cancer and is in great pain and needs an end to her suffering. She's not suffering; she doesn't even know what's going on. It's the other people that suffer. And even that isn't suffering; it's just an inconvenience. Is that a new plea for justifiable homicide? Inconvenience?"

"Aren't you being a little harsh?"

Carl started over. "Okay, let's say we understand why he did it. Let's say we forgive him. All I'm saying is I don't want him to do it again."

"Granted."

"Thank you."

"But are you sure he did it in the first place?"

"No. I'm not sure."

"So what are you going to do?"

It came down to that again.

"If you're right and she's out there lost, you can't just do nothing."

"And you're saying the police could find her."

"Well?"

"But if she's a ghost these are all moot questions."

"That's why I'm taking all of this so calmly," Kit said with a smile.

"Ackerman is covering something up, I'm sure of that much. Maybe I'm wrong about what it is. If I could be sure he's not going to hurt her, I'd call the police in a minute."

"How can you be sure?"

"I think he said his brother was on the boat that night."

"Really?"

"If I could talk to the brother and find out what really happened..."

"I have to say," Kit interrupted, "I find it hard to believe he'd kill his wife with his brother on the boat."

"Why? You're perfectly willing to believe she's a ghost."

"Well, I guess we all have different things we want to believe."

Carl had had enough. "What the fuck does that mean? Why should I want to believe that he tried to kill her?"

"I don't know, but you're sure fighting for it."

"I'm not fighting for anything. This isn't some story idea we're working on."

"Okay. Go on." He was granting Carl this insignificant point, waiting for the bigger prey to pounce on.

"He said when they went out on the boat she panicked because she'd forgotten she knew how to sail. Now that can't be true. She's only regressed, or whatever you call it, back to eighteen or nineteen years old. She's been sailing since she was ten."

"So?" Carl thought this was such an important point and the only response it got was a 'so?'

"Ackerman's brother was the one who used to sail with her, he was on the boat. I want to talk to him. Can you help me find him?"

Kit shook his head. "I'm just consulting on this. My advice is, go to the police, tell them how you feel and let them decide."

"The police won't give a fuck about how I feel."

"Make them care. Show them the check, that's bound to make them suspicious."

Carl felt an embarrassed blush. "I tore it up."

Kit reacted with surprising concern. "What?"

"It made me sick."

"That was a mistake." Kit was on his feet, thinking as he walked, like he always did when he was picking holes in a story. "I mean, right now he thinks you're a run-of-the-mill blackmailer and writes you off. But when he finds you didn't even cash the check, he's going to know there's more to it than that. I suppose you gave him your name?"

"Sure. But I didn't tell him anything else about me."

"Just your name?" Kit was already flipping through the damned phone book. There was only one Carl Robson. "But cheer up," Kit said, "maybe he won't think to look."

"You're worried too," Carl said.

"The check is a problem. I guess I'll find the brother. You don't know his name?"

"Sorry."

Kit threw the phone book down. "Then I have to actually work."

Carl caught Kit just as his car was pulling out of the driveway. Kit gave him his best patronizing look, but let him have his say.

"I was thinking about that letter from her little brother. He was supposed to be here just before she died, but in the letter he didn't seem to understand her problem. Ackerman tried to explain that away, but I don't think he was out here at all."

Kit considered. "Why would he lie about that?"

"I don't know, but it might be a good idea to talk to Jeff too. I wish there was a way to get in touch with him."

"In Peru?" Kit laughed. "Wait, I have some good contacts, I'll ask my lawn man."

Carl watched him drive off. He stood on the curb and looked up through the eucalyptus trees to the twilight sky. He went back into the house and put Bobby Brown and the Rhythm Aces on the CD player. The music sounded hollow and tinny, fighting against the silence of an empty house and losing. He cranked it. His father wasn't there to tell him to turn it down. "Searching, searching for my baby…" Carl turned it off in disgust.

EIGHT

The clock in the rented car read two a.m. Carl huddled in the front seat and missed the temperature button in his car. It was cold, but he'd feel warmer if he knew just how cold. He rubbed his arms and watched the huge, quiet, white house.

It's late for her to be out, he thought. If she looks at a clock, she'll think 'Oh, God, I've got to get home, my folks'll kill me, and she'll drive back here and he'll be waiting outside in his car to find her. If she looks at a clock. If she has the car. If she's free to come and go at will.

There could be any number of perfectly harmless reasons why she might not be able to make it back here tonight. Any number. And if she didn't, well, when the morning came, he could just go up to the house, leave his name and number and tell them to call if she shows up. They'd be glad to co-operate. They'd do anything to get rid of her.

And if she never did show up here? If he never saw her again, never heard from her? Would he find himself believing Kit's idea that she was an apparition? Even if it were true, why would she have come to him? To haunt him into avenging her murder? But remember the feel of her, he told himself. Remember the taste of her. She was real and she needed him.

He drifted off to sleep in the front seat and dreamed he was kissing her while she rotted in his arms.

He slept for about ten minutes before his door was flung open, someone grabbed his arm and yanked him out onto the street.

NINE

Four blocks away, in another silent house, Jenny Kallen was reading a letter by flashlight under the covers. Her parents were asleep, the whole world was asleep, but she could never join them. She could never join them in anything now, she was too far-gone. The feeling inside was too different, too powerful, too wicked to ever let her be like normal people again. Tomorrow would set them apart from everyone and probably destroy them both, but if it did it didn't matter. There was no denying it; there was no resisting it.

She would meet him tomorrow and she would be his. Tomorrow in the theater.

Carl was lifted off the pavement, shoved against the hood of the car and shaken once or twice before he had time to get confused.

"Who the hell are you?" The voice was loud and close to his face, the breath smelt of eggs.

Carl tried to look around the huge face that was barking so close to his. It was still nighttime. Jesse's house was still not there.

"What the hell are you up to?" The voice was still barking. "You want me to call the cops?"

Carl coughed weakly and tried to speak. "I'm just waiting for somebody."

He didn't listen. "You and your crazy girlfriend have just about scared my wife to death and if I see you around here one more time I'm not gonna waste my time with the police, I'm gonna start breaking fingers."

Carl admired the use of a specific image; his fingers were already clenched together, hoping to find safety in numbers.

"I didn't mean to scare you, I'm sorry. It's just that I can't find her."

"Who?"

"Jesse, the woman who came by here before."

"Who the hell is she?"

Carl searched around for an answer. "She's my wife," he lied. "She has this brain problem, she forgets things. She used to live here and she forgets she doesn't. I know she'll be back, she's bound to. Just let me give you my number, call when she comes. I promise you, it'll be the last time she comes back."

The man looked up at him, then relaxed his hold. Carl straightened up and looked at his assailant for the first time. He wasn't a really big man. Just an average guy in pajamas, driven to an average fury because someone had been bothering his wife. Don't mess with the loved ones, Carl thought, that brings out the monster in everybody.

He took the piece of paper Carl had scribbled his number on and pocketed it, then looked at Carl doubtfully. "You lost her, huh?" Carl nodded. "That's tough. I'll give you a call if we see her."

Carl thanked him profusely and got back in the car, keeping his eyes behind him and trying to figure out what to do if the hand grabbed him again. It didn't. He shut the door and started the engine.

The guy called out from the street, "You do have the cops looking for her, don't you?"

Carl drove off without answering.

TEN

There were three other cars in the high school parking lot – a black BMW, a black Mercedes and Ted's old Jeep. Jenny parked her mother's Chrysler next to the BMW. As if, she laughed to herself, parking next to Ted's car was too intimate.

She still had time to back out, she told herself. She looked at her face in the visor mirror. Not pretty, she knew that. She carried too much weight on her face. Her mousy hair wasn't blonde or brunette or red or any color with a name – it was just the color of hair. Her eyes bulged slightly – the contact lenses had been a mistake. At least her glasses had hidden that popeyed look. Her skin was all right, if you liked a fair, creamy complexion. She didn't. To her it looked pale and fishy.

How could anyone look at this face and feel anything? But he did.

And the way she'd dressed had been a real mistake. She fastened the buttons on her blouse which she had left daringly open this morning. She wasn't sexy, and trying to be only made her look ridiculous. No one could want her. But he did.

She was just an ordinary girl. Less than ordinary. A forgotten, plain girl. She couldn't make someone crazy. She couldn't break a heart or wreck a home. But she was going to.

Time to do it now, she told herself. Time to start the engine and drive home and forget the whole thing.

She opened the car door and started walking towards the school. Just for a second she was a romantic heroine, walking elegantly, in the jeans she filled perfectly, toward her assignation with destiny. The world would scorn her, society would reject her, but with a love as grand as theirs, it wouldn't matter what anyone said.

Then the second passed and she was a fifteen-year-old girl and she was very scared.

Ted Ryan's office was tucked away behind the backstage area. It was supposed to be a storage room, but the school's chronic office shortage had led to its conversion. Ted resented it at first, – the ultimate show of disrespect from the school to its drama teacher, shoving him away in a closet back there in the dark. But if it had been intended as an insult, he'd turned it on its head. The storeroom was now his secret enclave, his hidden court, his private domain.

It was bigger than anyone else's office and the bare cement walls, metal beams and exposed light bulbs gave it a boho personality. But best of all it was private, tucked away behind the double locked doors of the theater, enshrouded by heavy back fly curtains. It was the perfect place to get drunk with his students and discuss theater and existentialism and the First Lady and race relations and the rain forest and Kurt Cobain and who was sleeping with whom.

The brightness of the kids amazed him. Ryan was sure that people only said today's kids were shallow because they failed to observe them through the necessary filter of bourbon and pot. Most of the adults he knew needed about twenty minutes of mind-altering before they said anything worthwhile; why should kids be any different?

So the office gave him the opportunity to get to know the kids better. It gave him an opportunity to do any number of things he wouldn't have been able to do otherwise. Like ruin his life, he thought with a grim smile.

He was married, of course. He lived well on his meager salary and had long since stopped resenting his low place on the social totem pole. What profession was looked on with more patronizing pity than that of a high school teacher? Everyone had been to high school, of course. Everyone else had been eager to leave, and the fact that he was still there wasn't seen as a career choice as much as a failure, as if he'd been held back a grade or twenty.

If it hadn't been for his office he might have believed that himself. But the office was so far away from everything schoolish. It was a little world all by itself. And the evenings spent rehearsing the millionth production of Blithe Spirit or Our Town were all apart too. You weren't a teacher and they weren't students in those times and in that place. You were just people. And you got to know them, and in this world some of those kids were older and had seen more of life than he had.

But not Jenny. Jenny was a sweet, bright innocent young girl. And he could have her today if he chose.

He walked out of the office and into the darkness of backstage. The huge black curtains in the wings muffled his steps on the hard wood as he felt his way in darkness to the lighting booth.

Her innocence was no deterrent to him. My God, he told himself, she's fifteen and still a virgin. That was a miracle in this school and it couldn't last long. Better for her that her first should be somebody who knew what he was doing, someone who'd be careful, someone who really cared for her, than some idiot pimply faced jock in the back of his car who wasn't thinking about anything but a quick fuck.

And he did care for her. He thought about her constantly, could hardly keep his eyes off her in class. At night he dreamed about her, or at least he tried to. He certainly thought about her when half asleep and half awake. His dreams he never remembered.

She was so different from Laura. Laura was so worldly, so decadently mature. Jenny's innocent enthusiasm was like a breath of fresh air after all the time he'd spent with cynical Laura. Besides, Laura graduated last year.

He opened the wire cage of the light booth and stepped in. He pulled up the huge wooden lever on the ancient light board – unbelievable that they'd never given him the money for a new one – and the stage was flooded with lights, all focused on the single rehearsal couch, center stage.

There was a knock on the loading door. He could go to answer it, but he knew it was unlocked. Better to wait and see who it was.

The door opened slowly and Jenny entered. Ryan stepped back into the shadows and watched. Good God, she'd tried to put on something sexy. It looked ludicrous on her, but it touched him deeply. He knew how self-conscious she was, how she liked to hide herself in drab, loose fitting clothes. She must be feeling as foolish as she looked in those tight jeans and that blouse – and my God she was undoing the top button. He didn't know whether to laugh or cry. She was baring herself to him, risking humiliation, the thing she feared most. Lord, she must trust him.

And that look in her eye as she crossed the stage into the bright lights. That wary look, half-hoping, half-fearing she might see something new. It was that mass of contradictions that had made him fall in love with her. The timid frightened little thing that walks into the light of danger. She's an adventurer, he told himself, and I'm just a tired old love-smitten fool, willing to be everything she wants and everything she fears.

She sat on the sofa, looking straight into the darkness. Did she know he was there? He turned to walk out to her. He thought of turning down the lights. He'd turned them down for Laura, but then Laura had been through it all and was blasé about love, so he had to be the romantic; love is all about contrast. With a shy little thing like Jenny you kept all the lights on.

Jenny kept her eyes fixed in front of her for fear of seeing him and panicking, running, spoiling everything. She thought her heart would break if she saw him; break or burst. It was so wrong what she was doing here, so wrong in every way.

But he was such a good man, such a handsome, gentle man. So intelligent, so romantic. She loved him from the first time she saw him. Standing there on the stage, talking to the class in his beautiful gruff voice about art, about the power to move people. He cared so much. He had so much passion.

He could have been a great actor; she had no doubt of that. He'd be a movie star – no, that would be too cheap – he'd be a Broadway star, if it wasn't for that wife of his. Oh, he denied it, but she could see how she weighed him down with responsibilities and worries. So he had to teach at this stupid school and it broke his heart to give up all his dreams. She used to think she'd give anything to make up for the sadness in his soul.

And then the silly had gone and fallen in love with her. Jenny. It couldn't be possible. He must just feel sorry for her. But he said it was love and he wouldn't lie, not on purpose. And instead of making him happier, she'd just made him sadder, damn it. But she could make him happier now, she thought, with a wave of panic. She'd wanted him so long and now he wanted her. It was horrible, like a nightmare and a daydream all coming true. She realized with a wave of embarrassment that she was wet between her legs. All this talk of love, she thought bitterly, when maybe all it came down to was that.

She jumped suddenly when she realized he was next to her, sitting on the end of the sofa. Had he seen her squeeze her thighs together just then? It would be too awful if he had, he'd be so disappointed in her.

"I was afraid you'd come here," he said.

She nodded; there was no way she could talk. Her mind was crazy with the thought that he must know, that he could smell her scent. It seemed so strong to her, it seemed to fill the air around her with accusations.

"If you hadn't I might have gotten through this, but now...I suppose it had to happen sooner or later."

"What?" She tried to smile.

"Don't tease me, I couldn't bear it," there was such hurt in his eyes. "I'm a teacher, I've never felt anything like this before. Not for a student. Not for anyone. I'm taking my life in my hands, risking my marriage, my career. What are you risking? I'm just an adventure to you. In a year you won't even remember me."

It hurt too much. She reached out and grabbed his hand. "Don't say that."

He stood in front of her, blocking out the lights from above. "Then what are you going to risk?"

She spoke, barely above a whisper. "We could go someplace."

"And do what?"

She blushed. Why did he have to make her say it? "You could make love to me."

He laughed. She looked up startled. It was a friendly laugh, but she didn't see anything funny here.

"Is that it?" he said. "Is that all you can think about? I'm risking my life and all you want is a good fuck...What's the matter? You don't like the word? It's a good, solid, Saxon word, one of the oldest in the language, from before all that French and Latin shit got mixed in. Why don't you say it? Say it for me."

She said it.

"Good girl," he stroked her face with his hand. "You can't keep me waiting now."

"Where shall we go?"

"What's wrong with here?"

She was speechless for a moment. "But this is the school."

"If we get caught somewhere else I'm just as dead."

He moved closer to her. She flinched. "At least turn the lights off."

"But I'm a teacher, aren't I? If you're going to learn anything from this, you have to see what I'm doing."

She turned away. She would have gotten up to run, but he was standing too close to her. Not that he was holding her down of course, she was sure he wasn't doing that.

"I can't," she said.

She felt him relax, sighing. "Then this is just a game, you don't really care for me, is that it?"

"No, I care!" She said it quickly, without thinking.

"Do you really?" He took her hand and pulled it to him. "Feel that? That's how much I care."

ELEVEN

Kit kicked the lawn chair and Carl jerked out of it with a start. "You look like hell," Kit said.

Carl drooped over the side of the chair, his head resting on the back of his hand. He felt like he was about to break into pieces.

"Didn't you get any sleep last night?"

"I got some." He staggered to his feet and stumbled back into the house for some coffee. He stopped half way through the living room when his brain kicked in. "Did you find Ackerman's brother?"

"Yeah," Kit threw his notebook onto the coffee table. Carl snatched it up. "Now are you going to call the police?" Kit asked.

"Not until I talk to him. Want some coffee?"

"Bullshit, Carl, she's already been out there a whole night, what the hell do you think she's doing? The girl's as helpless as she can be."

"I thought she was a ghost."

"Knock it off. Think about her for once."

"She's all I'm thinking about."

"Oh, that's obvious. But what good is it doing her?"

"I'm trying to find her."

"Sure, but you're one guy and you don't know what you're doing. Let the cops look for her. They'll find her. After all she's not hiding and she does make a rather distinctive impression."

Carl sat down on the sofa. He hadn't changed since yesterday. He hadn't even been in the house. He'd just climbed out of the car and collapsed into the lawn chair. He wiped his face with his hand; his skin felt like it was coated with a layer of grease.

"What did you find out about the brother?"

"His name is Frank Ackerman, works in his brother's firm. Don't get the feeling he's much of a live wire. More nepotism in action. Oh, and he was also Jesse's lover for the past two years."

Carl sat bolt upright.

"Are you sure?"

"Well, you can never know the truth for sure, but when you tap into the secretarial gossip pool you get closer to it than anywhere else."

Carl was on his feet now, pacing restlessly. "Well, that's it then. There's a real motive. Not only is she an invalid, but he resents her for being unfaithful. Sure you don't want some coffee?"

Carl was heading for the kitchen when Kit spoke. "You know what I don't like about this? How happy you sound."

Carl stopped and turned back. "Of course I'm not happy. It's horrible, but it is a relief to get closer to the truth. I'm getting coffee."

As he moved he noticed the red light blinking on his answering machine. He played back the message. One from Kit, wondering where he was. Then one other.

"Carl, this is Martin Ackerman. I don't know what the hell I was thinking yesterday, but I canceled payment on that check. You can choke on it. Try to pull anything like that again, I'll have my lawyers on you. Fuck yourself."

Carl started at the machine, bewildered. He didn't notice that Kit was at his side till he heard him dialing the phone.

"Hello, I'd like to report a missing person."

Carl's hand hit the cradle, cutting the connection. "What are you doing?" he asked.

"Well, that's it, isn't it?" Kit said. "I mean this whole thing was based on the idea he was paying you for keeping some deep dark secret. Now he isn't. He was just confused. You got nothing to worry about."

"Let me talk to the brother first."

"There's no point. Nobody's hiding anything any more. Let the cops find her for God's sakes, before…"

"Let me talk to the brother!"

"Fuck the brother! What's the matter with you? She needs help."

"I'm going to talk to him, I'm going to find out for sure."

"You want there to be some mystery, don't you? You just want an excuse to keep her all to yourself, with everybody thinking she's dead, so you can keep on playing your little teen-age love game."

Carl walked in silence to the coffee maker and finally poured his cup. "Jesus, this isn't about me sleeping with somebody," he said quietly.

"So you haven't slept with her?"

"No."

"Fine, lie if you want to."

"Kit, I just want to make sure he's not going to hurt her. As soon as I know that, I'll call…"

"Don't try to pretend like you're acting reasonable, Carl, because you're doing anything but. Now I know you've been lonely lately. Everyone's aware of this depression you've been going through…"

"Don't fucking psychoanalyze me." He set his cup down with a crack. "And what the hell's wrong with being depressed anyway? Who made that a crime?"

"Fine, I can't live your life for you." Kit got up to go. "You coming into work later?"

Carl looked shocked. "No."

"Why not?"

"I think this is more important than a stupid TV show."

"It's your career."

"Sorry. I think this is more important than my stupid career."

"I'm not going to lie for you."

"Then don't."

"I'm not sure Don and Mindy will understand…"

"Then tell them I quit."

"You can't quit, you're my partner."

"So sue me."

"Look, I know you're defensive about the idea of therapy…"

"Just leave me alone."

Kit settled on the counter, fiddling with his cup, ready for a long talk. "I'm telling you, you're behaving just like I did before I went into recovery from cocaine. Anger, denial. I just don't know what you're addicted to."

Carl walked to the door and opened it. "Get out."

"Hey, I'm not the problem."

"Get out."

Kit displayed his palms in patient supplication. "I'm trying to be serious."

"Kit, I don't want to have to hit you."

"Why not?"

"Because I don't know how. But I'm willing to learn." He crossed to Kit, grabbed his arm and pulled him to the door.

"What are you doing?" Kit was shocked.

"I'm throwing you out."

Carl opened the door. Kit stood on the threshold, his brow furrowed in irritation. "You know you're not throwing me out."

Carl put his hand on Kit's shoulder and shoved him so that he stumbled off balance. Kit brushed Carl's hand away with a quick, bug-slapping gesture. "Get your hand off me."

Carl swung the hand up again and shoved. Kit stumbled out the door, tried to find his footing and tripped on the stoop, flailing back against the railing. He was on his feet again in a second, stepping up to the door. Carl slammed it in his face.

"All right," Kit called out. "Fuck you. Fuck me for trying to help you. Fuck me!" Kit kicked the door, took a few steps down the driveway, turned back and yelled, "Fuck me!" Then he walked the rest of the way to his car.

Carl leaned against the door, his eyes shut, his hands shaking. This stupid shoving match was the closest he'd come to violence since he was in grade school, and it left the blood pounding in his temples.

Not that any of it made Kit wrong, of course. If Ackerman wasn't paying him off, Ackerman wasn't hiding anything. And if Ackerman wasn't hiding anything, what was all this about?

He should call the police then. He should call Kit and apologize. He should go to work and forget all about this.

He picked up the phone and called Frank Ackerman.

TWELVE

As soon as he set foot in Frank Ackerman's house, Carl knew why he had felt uncomfortable, so disappointed, in Martin Ackerman's house. Carl had gone to Martin's house expecting to find where Jesse had lived. He'd looked for signs of her, traces of her, the scent of the girl he'd known. All he'd found was an interior decorated, see-how-much-money-I'm-making trophy. He hadn't expected her to grow up that shallow.

But now he knew. That hadn't been her house. She'd lived here, with Frank. Even if, as Frank told him, she'd only been able to steal a few hours out of the week to spend here, still this was her home.

Here were the sun-filled windows, the honest sloppiness, the colors, the flowers, the knickknacks, the sense of fun. The game boards hung on the walls in place of art, the scattered Cary Grant videos, the old vinyl records and homemade cassette tapes. The smell of Jesse.

Not that she'd had backgammon boards on her walls when Carl had known her. Not that videotapes had even existed back in the pre-home entertainment 70s. But Frank's Jesse was Carl's Jesse. His things were things Jesse would have grown to love, if she had grown older…which, of course, she had.

The music scattered about under Carl's feet in those self-labeled cassettes that fit the picture well. It wasn't Jesse's music from '75, but it was music that followed through on that music. If she'd listened to Linda Ronstadt singing "Don't Cry Now" and actually thought it was cutting edge (or whatever the cutting edge term for cutting edge was back then), it was right and proper that she be listening to Mary-Chapin Carpenter now. Jackson Browne then, John Gorka now. Loudon Wainright then, Jonathan Richman now. Emmylou Harris then, Emmylou Harris now.

But the biggest clue that this place was Jesse's home was the simplest one; Carl felt at home here.

And Frank, much as he resisted it at first, was one of the reasons he felt that way. Carl didn't know what he'd expected – someone cold, like Martin? Some easy-to-hate Lothario, who'd corrupted her? Doubtless simple jealousy had led him to expect (hope?) to dislike the man.

But from the initial phone conversation, any such expectations had been doomed to disappointment. Frank had invited this stranger to his house to talk about Jesse without suspicion and with at least a good imitation of true hospitality. It was positively un-Los Angelino.

Frank lived in the Arroyo Seco on the Pasadena side, just under the Colorado Street Bridge. Carl loved driving that bridge. The blonde masonry, the delicate, yet ornate arches, the way the structure curved, gently, to catch the far hill like an oncoming wave, made it one of the most beautiful bridges in the world. John Barrymore had leapt to freedom from this bridge, escaping from his police inspector brother Lionel, in the old picture Arsene Lupin – but in the film the bridge had been in France in that story and, presumably, had spanned water.

A huge expansive freeway crossed the same arroyo at almost the same spot, about twenty feet over, rendering the Colorado essentially obsolete. But for once, beauty survived.

Frank's house was another piece from the past – a little Arts and Crafts bungalow, just under the shadow of the bridge. But old things, as Carl was soon to discover, were Frank's passion. "I'm a new-o-phobe," he said. "If it was made in my life time, I'm very suspicious of it. If it was made since the Ford Administration, it's got to be shit."

Carl was pulling into the driveway when he first saw Frank – mid-thirties, wiry, wearing an old t-shirt and jeans and apparently using some bizarre garden tool to trim the Wisteria that entwined the porch. Carl was about to break the ice by asking what the hell kind of clipper that was, when he realized it was a prosthetic arm. Frank's real right arm ended just below the elbow. Leave it to Kit to fail to mention a detail like that.

Carl was able to pull his eyes away from the hook just as Frank stepped forward offering his left hand to shake. "Excuse the hand," he said, smiling, "I'd shake with my right but I can't remember where the hell I left it." Carl liked him right away.

In the living room, (all cluttered, warm, and Jesse), Marcia Ball was howling on the cassette player, getting all garbled and sour – the tape was being eaten by the machine. Frank pulled the cassette out, black tape trailing behind it, like jellyfish tentacles. "Disemboweled another one," he said. "Good music always dies young."

He crossed to his turn table (Carl couldn't remember when he'd last seen one of those) and put on an old black vinyl Eagles record. He moved the arm in position and dropped it – there was that so familiar and yet forgotten explosion, the 'pow' of sound from the needle hitting the vinyl. Then the traveling noises, the hisses and pops and crackles as the needle made its way to the first groove. So much music and the record hadn't even started yet.

When Carl asked if he ever thought about getting a CD player, Frank shook his head vigorously. "Don't believe in 'em. They don't get scratches. You can't effect them. They don't change from you listening to them. There's no relationship there."

"When my first girlfriend left me, I was in high school and I just listened to that Beatles song "For No One." I just listened to it over and over again. Played it to death, as they say. But you really could do that. That song deteriorated, it wasted away. It didn't just communicate Paul McCartney's pain, it felt my pain. It got so you had to put a quarter on the arm just to make it play. If I were to put it on for you now, you could still hear the heartache. But the CD? You just hear four guys in a recording studio somewhere."

He handed Carl a Mexican beer and a lime, saying, "You're going to have to say something or I'm just going to keep talking. I haven't seen another human being for two weeks."

Carl swallowed, wondering if he'd do a better job of bringing up the topic with this Ackerman. "I want to talk about Jesse."

"Come on."

Frank didn't hesitate. He led Carl through the kitchen, past pictures of circus performers and antique magic posters ("The Amazing Morton Wonder Show – Totally different from all other Ghost Shows"), and into the back yard.

A riot of colors out there. Roses blooming wildly in huge human-head sized blossoms. "These were her babies. I mean, they were here long before I moved in, but she turned them into this. She taught me how to cut them back. She was vicious at it. Really, you'd have thought she killed the poor things. But then they came back for her, just like this. Almost violent.

"My bedroom's down in the basement – very unusual for a house like this to have a full basement – and she used to stand there nude on her tip toes, looking out the ground level window there, trying to spot the aphids, she used to say, when they didn't know she was looking." He cupped one of the massive blossoms in his hand. "Best crop she had. She'd have loved it." His voice trailed off and for the first time, he looked sad.

He shook it off with a quick smile. "So, what did you want to know?"

Her nude at the window, that brought back a little of Carl's jealousy. But nude aphid spotting? It was hard not to like that. "Well, there's so much. I haven't seen her for years."

"Yeah, I know."

"She mentioned me?"

"Sure. You always go through that, don't you? What's your favorite movie? Your favorite song? Was your first lover kind?"

"What did she say?"

"Annie Hall, 'Who Knows Where the Time Goes,' and yes."

"Really?"

"Are you surprised?"

"To be honest, yeah," Carl laughed.

"Well, there was that too," Frank laughed as well, "but she remembered you fondly, in spite of...whatever. I think if you'd given her a call sometime, she would've gotten a real kick out of it."

Carl didn't answer right away. Why had he never made that call? Because he could never find the words to make it right? Well, now, of course, there was no need. "I always meant to."

"Well...we all mean to do things."

And then there was one of those silences Carl hated. It took a special kind of man to let conversation dry up in just this way. Women, he imagined, might hug and cry at a moment like this, though he'd never actually seen that happen. Other kinds of men, Slavs and Italians, you know, the ethnic types, might be able to cry and drink and sing old songs in minor keys. Rednecks might punch each other a few times and then go hunt something. But his type of man, HomoSuburbius, could only sit awkwardly and look for a way to change the subject.

Fortunately, Carl had one easily to hand. "Anyway, when I heard what happened...and what was in the papers was so sketchy...you were there weren't you?" So he'd gotten to the point after all, if only to end an embarrassing moment.

Frank nodded.

So...take the plunge, boy, Carl told himself. "Did it happen like they said in the paper?"

"Did what happen?"

"The accident."

Frank took another sip from his beer. "Oh. It was no accident," he said and his smile was as brief as a heartbeat.

THIRTEEN

Carl had to remind himself to breathe while he waited for Frank to go on.

Frank leapt to his feet so suddenly that Carl almost toppled off his chair. "There's something I have to show you, do you mind?"

Back in the kitchen, Frank pulled out a big box containing a half dozen framed photographs.

"I used to want to be a professional photographer, but the industry blacklisted me just because I had no talent, which is very un-American, don't you think?"

Carl laughed, recognizing his own kind of joke. We must be her type, Carl realized. He could almost see Jesse's personal ad, "Attractive woman looking for insecure, self-deprecating under-achiever with good sense of humor and a love of oral sex."

"I used to have these up, but..." Frank pulled out a few pictures. Nothing too special from a creative point of view. Just black and white shots of Jesse in front of her roses, her skin blindingly white against the grey roses. A too posed shot of her in cowboy boots leaning on a road sign (pitted by the ubiquitous shot gun blast), reading Borrego Springs, the look in her eye just slightly suggestive. Odd, he thought, she looks older in these pictures than she does in life. Remembering her alive seemed strange in this setting and he wondered if Kit was right and she was a ghost after all.

"She really grew into a remarkable person. I wish you could have known her," Frank said, closing the box. And Carl realized that there was another Jesse he'd never known, never would know. The woman Jesse had become. And that Jesse really was dead, he thought, a sense of loss washing over him.

"But what about the accident?" he ploughed on.

"Well, the boat trip was my idea. She'd always liked sailing, and I thought...Wait." He stopped and looked up at Carl, concerned. "You know she was sick, don't you?"

Carl told him he knew, but he gave no details. Some kind of brain disorder, he said. Some kind of amnesia.

Frank went into detail. Describing all the symptoms Carl knew only too well. Carl wanted to stop him, to tell him he didn't have to go through it all again, but no, not yet. There was more to discover.

"Of course, she forgot we were having our affair. That came early on. That was a bitch...It had taken so long to get there in the first place and then...it was all erased." He pulled himself up in his chair. "Martin and I were always trying to jog her memory. The doctors told us that was helpless but, well, it was something to do. Otherwise, we'd go mad. And I suppose we'd seen so many TV shows and movies where something, the right piece of music, a conk on the head, brings someone's memory back, that we just couldn't believe it was impossible."

"So, I said take her out on the boat. I thought she'd remember the boat or the feeling of sailing, at least. Maybe that would help. It didn't. She still didn't know who we were. She was alone out there on the sea with these strangers. Terrified. I tried to talk to her like I always did, to remind her of things. She didn't know me. Finally I got angry and I went below, just for a few minutes, just to cool off. When I came back she was gone. Just gone. We looked, we searched but...it was as if she'd never been there."

Carl felt a little deflated.

"So it was an accident."

Frank set his beer down on the table. "No. How do you think an able bodied woman falls off a sail boat in the middle of a calm sea?"

"So what are you saying?"

He looked around the room, irritated, like someone who is asked to explain a joke. "She was trying to escape...from us."

Carl still wasn't satisfied.

"Was your brother with you when you went below?"

"No, he was reading on the bow."

"Did you see him?"

"No."

"So he could have left, gone up on deck, and..."

"And thrown her in? Yes. I've thought of that. I like that better than her killing herself to get away from me."

"But you don't believe it?"

He shook his head, sadly. "Why would he do it?"

"Did he know you and Jesse were lovers?"

Frank laughed. "Well, I've never met you and you know, so I suppose it's a fair bet that he knew. Yes, he knew. And he was very understanding, very noble about it. My brother's very understanding and noble about most things."

"But you don't think, out of jealousy..."

"No, not jealousy. You have to care to be jealous."

"But what kind of life did he have ahead of him, tied to her?"

"Yes, that's better. Killing for convenience."

"Do you think he might have?"

Frank met his eyes. "Well, it's better than the truth. Why do you care so much?"

"Because it doesn't add up. Trying to escape? Where to? I don't care how disoriented she was, she knows where she is at any given moment, she's not going to jump into open..."

Frank cut him off with sudden intensity. "How do you know how she is?"

There were a lot of questions Carl might have asked himself before he spoke. He asked none of them. "She's alive," he said.

FOURTEEN

When she opened her eyes a bright light flooded in, spreading from below all around her. She sat up and looked at her strange surroundings in confusion. A bare concrete ceiling encrusted with dust only a few feet above her head. Metal supports branching from it to the floor just beneath her. She shifted and felt a splinter in her leg. She was on a rough plywood platform that stretched forward all the way to the source of the light – a long slit in the floor that was so blazingly bright she could hardly look at it.

Then she realized that it wasn't the floor beneath her at all, it was the ceiling. She laughed at her own confusion. She was up in the ceiling above the auditorium, of course. But why the hell had she been sleeping up here? Hell of a place for a nap, she thought with a laugh. Then she stopped and grabbed the railing a little tighter. What if she'd rolled over in her sleep? Everyone does that. She was always rolling over on her cat in bed. What if she'd rolled over and right off this board in her sleep, waking up in mid air, wondering why she was falling, too late to do anything? God, that would have been horrible.

But it hadn't happened, she told herself, climbing to her feet. She was okay and she'd never be stupid enough to nap here again, that was for sure. Once she made it to the lights she'd know what was going on. Someone was obviously working on the stage or the lights wouldn't be on. It would be Floyd or Mr. Ellison or Carl and once she saw them she'd remember why the hell she'd come up here. Hell, she'd probably just dozed off for a second, not long enough to do any fatal rolling.

At the thought of Carl she felt a little guilty again. She really should tell him, she really had to. It wasn't like it was something that was going to go away. Could that be why she was here? Was she planning to meet him here for a private talk? They'd come here once before she remembered with a grin. During lunch they'd sneaked through the trap door and made love right there, right in school, with everyone all around them and no one suspecting. Except maybe Annie, she'd seen them sneak out afterward and rolled her eyes, but in a nice way. She'd liked the idea. Annie was a romantic too.

She made it to the lights. The catwalk here was much broader, the railing was made of metal and she felt perfectly safe now. This was her turf. She crouched next to the lights – they were blazing with heat and she had to squint to keep them from blinding her, even though they were pointing away from her, down onto the stage. She might have called out now, but she waited for her eyes to adjust, so she could see who was down there and know whose name to call.

The pain in her eyes eased. She was a good thirty feet up, so it took her a moment to spot them; two figures on the sofa, center stage. She didn't know them and at first she thought they were working on a scene. Then she realized they were fucking.

She didn't say anything – if it was her down there she wouldn't want to be interrupted. But she didn't turn away either. She didn't mean to watch, it was just that she'd never seen anyone doing this before. It certainly wasn't a turn on, in fact the whole thing looked so absurd she couldn't believe it felt as good as it did. But maybe it wasn't feeling so good for them – that couldn't be how she and Carl looked when they did it.

She started to turn away, wondering how long she was going to have to wait up here for them to be through, when she heard a sound and then she knew she and Carl had never looked like that. She heard the girl crying.

She turned to look again. She could hear the girl whimpering. She'd pulled away and was curled up at one end of the sofa. Jesse didn't recognize either of them. What the hell were these strangers doing in the auditorium?

"I can't," the girl said. The acoustics of the theater were such that Jesse could hear her perfectly.

"Sure, you can. You can do anything." The guy had a confident tone, a fatherly tone. He bent over to kiss her and Jesse could see that he wasn't a student. He was a man, at least twenty years older than the girl. Jesse felt sick.

"No, it hurts."

"Come on, it always hurts at first. It'll feel good, trust me."

"But it doesn't, you said that and it doesn't. I just can't relax. I gotta go."

She started to stand up and he took her hand. Jesse could tell the girl was surprised by how tight he was holding it.

"You can't leave me like this," he said. "Not when you're the one who brought me here. Think about the risks I've been taking."

She started crying now, really crying. "I'm sorry, Ted, but I can't. I gotta go home."

He stood up, holding on to her arms. Not that she was going to run, not that she had the strength to run. "You can't leave a man like this. You have to learn that."

"But I really don't think I should do this. I changed my mind."

"How can you do that? Don't you even care about me?"

She sat down again, her face in her hands. The man walked around her and started rubbing her shoulders. "You know I'd let you go if you really wanted to. But I don't think you do. I don't think you're that selfish."

The girl laid her head back on the sofa and wiped her eyes and nose. She looked over at him and Jesse didn't think she'd ever seen a face that looked that young.

"Isn't there…something else I could do?"

The man laughed and sat on the back of the sofa. "What did you have in mind?"

She didn't laugh. "I don't know. I don't know how."

He slid down next to her and took her head in his hands. "I'll teach you. Will you let me teach you?"

"Yes," she answered with a lifeless voice.

There are some things you can't see when you're in the middle of them, Jesse thought. There are some things you can only see thirty feet up, leaning over a tungsten lamp.

He was pulling the girl's head toward his lap when Jesse kicked a lamp with a loud rattle and yelled out, "Get your hands off her, you pervert!"

They both jumped and tried to cover themselves – the man pulling his pants up, the girl trying to climb into the sofa. Jesse might have laughed if she hadn't been so angry.

The girl was too scared to cry now. "Who's there?" she asked.

"It's not what you think," the man said and Jesse did have to laugh, wondering what the hell else it could be.

"Put your dick back in your pants and leave that kid alone."

The girl started crying again – Jesse was starting to find it annoying.

"Girl, get your clothes on and get out of here."

The man had his pants zipped up and was recovering his dignity. He squinted up into the glare of the lights, trying to catch a glimpse of his discoverer.

"Who are you? What are you doing up there? This is a county building."

Jesse laughed again, amazed at his gall. If she hadn't been thirty feet up and hidden from sight she might have found him intimidating.

The girl had gathered her clothes up and was stumbling for the fire exit. The man followed her.

"I can't let you go like this, let me take you home."

"Leave her alone, Ted," Jesse said, in her sternest voice.

"Will you shut up?" he said. "Can't you see you're upsetting her?"

"I'm okay, really," the girl said. She tried to pull herself together and Jesse was getting downright pissed at her, because she knew the girl was doing it for his sake.

"_I'm_ upsetting her? What the fuck were you doing?" Jesse called out.

The man walked back center stage and looked up at the lights; he wasn't squinting now. "Now you come down here and you leave quietly and I promise you I won't call the police."

"The police? Go ahead, how does the phrase statutory rape grab you? How about a few years in prison, pervert?"

The girl turned her head into one of the curtains. Jesse wondered when the fuck she was going to put her clothes on.

"You don't know us. You have no right to try to turn this into something ugly." He was defiant now, glorying in his argument. Jesse wished she could spit far enough to reach him. She could imagine how scary a man like that could be if you were close to him, if you thought he knew best. Thank God she was far enough away to feel like God.

"Well, it looked real pretty from here. What are you her uncle?"

"I'm a teacher at this school and I have a right to be here, the question is who the hell are you?"

"A teacher! Oh, this is great, Mr. Doran's going to love that."

"Who is Mr. Doran?"

Jesse laughed again. "The principal, and you'd know that if you were really a teacher. Now you leave her alone and get the hell out of here..." The sentence dwindled off because she suddenly realized she was getting to a 'before I' do something, and she had no idea what she could do.

He looked up at her for a long while. He seemed to know where she was now and to stare straight at her. They both seemed to be having the same thought at the same time: She was up there, and there was no way down that wasn't past him.

He was very calm when he spoke. "Young lady, are you going to come down or am I going to have to come up and get you?"

FIFTEEN

He spent a long time waiting for an answer. He thought he heard a movement up there, but it was so far away it was hard to tell. He kept searching his memory, trying to place that voice, but nothing came to him.

There was no ladder, no scaffolding for her to have climbed. That meant she must have used that old passageway inside the lighting booth. No one had been allowed up there in all Ryan's time at the school. Years ago, students had actually been permitted to climb around in there, until a boy had fallen through the ceiling and hit the linoleum floor thirty feet below. Since then the place had been locked up – lighting adjustments were made by the custodial staff on the scaffolding. He'd barely glanced at the trapdoor himself.

Still, he'd heard rumors of students exploring when no one was watching, using it as a hiding place for pot smoking and God knew what all. Sometimes he'd find the trapdoor unlocked, but he never investigated; he didn't think it was his place to patrol the insides of the building. He had more important jobs to do.

So this was one of those wild students, probably stoned silly, trying to scare him. Well, she'd succeeded. But why couldn't he place the voice?

He turned back to Jenny and helped her get dressed. She was still crying and she was no help at all, limp in all the wrong places.

"What are we going to do?" Jenny asked.

"I got this buttoned wrong, will you help?"

"What are we going to do? Mom's not going to find out, is she?"

He pulled her behind the black curtain and grabbed her arms, tightly. "Listen stupid, your mother's not the problem. This is serious, stop acting like a kid."

She wiped her eyes and tried to stand up straighter. "I'm sorry. Could they really send you to jail?"

"I think so."

"Oh, God I'm so sorry."

He held her and stroked her hair. "That's okay, it'll work out. But you're gonna owe me a good one." He laughed.

"Yeah, whatever you say." She tried to laugh too.

"Now you can't go home."

She winced. "Oh, God."

"Now you gotta stand by me. We just have to talk to her. I'm sure this kid doesn't want to hurt anybody."

She nodded quickly and silently.

"Good girl. Now you just back me up."

A loud rattling sound split the silence of the stage. Ryan and Jenny ran to the lighting cage – the trapdoor was shaking. Ryan knelt down next to it, shifting a large metal shelf filled with lighting gels to have more room.

"It's locked," he spoke to the girl behind the door, calmly, helpfully.

The rattling stopped.

"I have the key. And I'll let you out if you promise not to make any trouble."

"Please," Jenny added.

A voice came from behind the door. "So you can go out and fuck some more little girls? How many have you fucked so far?"

Jenny was at the door to the cage, she turned away at that.

"My name is Ted, and this is Jenny. What's your name?" His voice was pure friendship and reason.

There was a pause. "Jessica."

"How old are you Jessica?"

"Eighteen. A little over the hill for you, I guess."

"Well, are you a little girl? I don't think so. You know as well as I do that high school kids today aren't children. Hell, they're more mature than most of the teachers. Wouldn't you say?"

She didn't answer.

He went on. "Now Jenny and I feel for each other very deeply. I know it's unconventional, but I respect her and I think she's old enough to make her own decisions. So you have a decision to make and I want you to think about it, because, if you wanted to, you could wreck my career, send me to jail, ruin my life and Jenny's too. And why? Because we were trying to find a little happiness. Is that what you want to do?"

"I don't know," there was a mocking edge to the voice that he was starting to hate, "but I don't think she wanted to fuck you and I know she didn't want to suck your dick."

He slammed on the door with his fist. "Don't talk like that in front of her, you bitch!"

The voice didn't stop. "Well, Jenny, did you want to fuck him? Did you?"

He turned to Jenny. She was outside the cage now, staring through the chicken wire. "Well," she said, "I really care for him…"

Ryan was at her in a second. "You don't have to justify yourself to that…" He faced the door again. "We don't have to justify anything. I can call the cops and have you arrested for trespassing and it'll be your word against ours. No matter what you say, Jenny will not turn on me."

"Maybe not, but I bet she's a lousy liar."

Ryan leaned against the door of the cage and looked back at Jenny. Does she look like a good liar, he asked himself. "Get out of here," he whispered.

"I want to help."

"Get out of here."

Jenny called out to the hated trapdoor, "I <u>did</u> want to fuck him."

Ryan grabbed her arm and shoved her toward the door. "Shut up! Haven't you done enough damage already? Now, get the fuck out of here."

She was out the door, but she stood there in the parking lot hesitating stupidly. "When will I see you?"

He slammed the door on her without answering. He hurried into his office and opened his filing cabinet. He pulled out a little plastic baggie filled with pot and a small film container filled with amphetamines. He ran into the boy's room across the hall from the auditorium and flushed them down the toilet. He sat on the lavatory floor with his head in his hands, feeling like he was trying to shove his brain back in place.

For the last two years he'd been walking a crazy tightrope, doing stupid, self-destructive things. He'd been miserably unhappy, stuck in a foolish marriage and a dead end job. So he'd flirted with danger in the most obvious ways. Doing drugs on the job, with his students – though that had seemed only fair since they were supplying the drugs. Fooling around with under aged girls, four of them by now, daring the world to catch him.

Well, now he was caught and suddenly he wanted to take it all back. He'd never thought about what it might mean. Oh, he'd pictured disgrace and looked forward to the messy dissolution of his marriage, but this was a crime. If this went wrong, and it wouldn't have to go <u>too</u> wrong, it could mean prison. And prison as a child molester. Oh, he knew that wasn't what he was, but that's what it would say, in black and white, in the papers, for everyone to read, for his mother to read, for God's sake. And he wouldn't be able to stand prison, it would kill him, it would kill him sure as anything.

He felt something wet on his tongue and realized he was crying. He stood up and pulled a brown paper towel from the dispenser and wiped his face. He walked back to the auditorium and glanced down the hall as he did so. There was no one there, no one else in the whole school. Oh, football practice would start in the gym in a few hours, but that was on the other side of the building. He opened the door and walked back onto the cool stage.

He crossed to the cage and sat down on the floor by the trap door again.

"Well, you're right," he whispered, "I can't call the police. What do you want me to do?"

There was no answer.

"I mean it, I'll give you anything I can. And I promise I'll never do it again. Just don't say anything, okay?"

There was no answer.

This wasn't fair of her. On top of everything else she shouldn't tease him.

"Okay?" He asked again.

He rattled the door. Again there was no response. He took the key from the top of the metal shelf and unlocked the padlock. He took a deep breath, then swung the door open.

There was no one in there.

SIXTEEN

He dropped the trapdoor shut again and leaned against the light board. She was gone. Had it finally happened; had he ignored a problem and seen it just go away? Maybe she really had been afraid of his threats after all. It was possible. Maybe she'd decided turning him in was too much trouble. That would be just like kids today. They had no sense of moral integrity, bless them.

But how had she gotten out? He wasn't sure, but he didn't think there was another way out of that place. Maybe she was still hiding up there, waiting for him to go away.

He walked to the center of the stage and looked up at the lights. They were too blinding for him to see anything around them. He went back into the booth and turned them down, then looked again. Nothing to see up there, but with so many shadows how could he know for sure?

He called out, "Are you there?"

No answer.

She had gone. He didn't have a thing to worry about. Of course, she might have gone to the police, but would they believe her? The first thing she'd have to admit when she told her story was that she'd broken into the place. He'd say he found her there and had threatened to call the police – or make that threatened to call her mother, that sounds much more understanding. Then she said he'd better not or she'd tell this ridiculous story. He'd just laughed and tried to talk sense to her. Then she ran off and to tell the truth he'd forgotten about the whole thing, it was so absurd. The police would believe him. Oh, they'd have to ask a few questions, talk to Jenny...

Ryan started to sweat again.

Jenny would lie, but that bitch was right, she wouldn't lie well. And, God save him, she might get some idea of helping him, saying something they hadn't agreed on. Even if she didn't, there'd be this look in her eye, they'd know she was hiding something.

Damn him, why had he picked her anyway? Now Laura, there was a girl who could lie with conviction. Between Laura and him, this chick in the ceiling would be expelled and on probation in no time. What had possessed him to fall for an innocent like Jenny this time? Good lord, for the first time he realized that this was the sort of girl who might even get depressed and tell her mother what was going on.

Then what would happen? The mother would make her turn on him. And then what? What if she testified? Jenny could really look like a child when she wanted to. He could picture her sitting on the witness stand, crying and whining about how he'd seduced her, maybe even saying a few nice things about him that would only make it all sound worse. And they'd all believe her, and what could he say? "Gentlemen of the jury you haven't seen her play the woman. You haven't had her giving you the eye, egging you on. You haven't seen her naked." They'd put him in prison.

Losing his job, his wife, his friends, that all might be something of a relief. But prison. And he'd heard how they treated child predators there; he'd heard it many times.

He heard someone stirring up in the ceiling.

"Is somebody down there?" she called out.

He didn't answer. He walked, as quietly as he could, back into the lighting booth. He picked the padlock off the floor and latched the trapdoor shut again.

He sat back against the metal cabinet and waited for her to come down. He lit a cigarette and listened. He could hear her scrambling around up there, like an oversized rat. She called out again, "Is anybody there? Floyd? Carl?"

He felt a twinge of worry – were there more of them? A whole gang of them up there, perhaps? But no, if she'd come with anyone they'd deserted her now. He took another drag on the cigarette, thinking that he'd quit soon. Quit smoking and drinking. And no more students, he'd swear off them for good. Especially the bad liars.

The trapdoor jarred. He jumped when he saw it and dropped the cigarette onto his lap. He snatched it up quickly, without a sound. He could hear her on the other side. "What the fuck?" she asked.

The door shook again. He saw the tips of her fingers probe under the door, feeling the latch. The door shook once more, even more violently this time. Now she was kicking it and he watched the latch with apprehension. Just how strong was it? He wondered as he watched it vibrate and rattle.

It was as if she hadn't expected it to be locked. But what would have made her think he'd leave it open? The kicking stopped, dwindled down to a few ineffectual punches. He heard her heavy breathing, heard a little whimper. She was getting tired of being in there. He put out his cigarette and leaned close to the door.

"You ready to talk now?" he whispered.

"Who's that?" There wasn't any fear in her voice, only relief. That annoyed him.

"It's Ted. Now do you want me to let you out?"

"Oh, thank God. Who the hell put a lock on this thing anyway?"

She was teasing him, he thought, bitterly. Asking pointless questions, refusing to be intimidated, even though she knew he had her trapped.

"Knock it off! Now are you ready to talk?"

There was a pause, then she answered in a doubtful voice, "Sure."

"You're not going to the police."

There was an even longer pause, then, "No, of course not."

"I want to believe you, I really do. Can you think of any way for me to be sure?"

Pause. "Cross my heart and hope to die."

He smacked the door with his fist. "Don't laugh at me! I could leave you in there. It's a three day weekend, do you want to be in there another two and a half days?"

"No," she answered quickly enough this time.

"All right then. Tell me how I can be sure you won't say anything."

"I won't, I won't say a word."

"Don't lie to me. Even if you don't go to the police, you'll tell your friends, and rumors will start spreading and then all some-body has to do is ask Jenny and it's all over…Not that I'm worried about myself, it's Jenny, it would destroy her, she's too young… Fuck it, I'm not going to prison. Now tell me, does anybody know you're here?"

Another pause, then, "Yes, a lot of people, my mother, my brother, my boyfriend…"

"You're not such a good liar yourself."

She shifted around in there, trying to pry open the door a bit more. He slapped it shut.

"Listen," she said, "you have to believe what I'm going to say, I really don't have any idea what you're talking about. I can't go to the police, I don't know anything, I don't know who you are or who Jenny is, I don't have anything to tell anybody. I think maybe you got me confused with somebody."

"How many people are up there?"

"Please believe me, I don't have any idea what you're talking about!"

"Shut up, it's too late for that."

He stepped out of the booth to get away from her whining. He walked about in the black curtains, thinking about those names she'd called. Floyd. Carl. Did they know she was here? It didn't seem likely, if they really knew wouldn't she have used their names just now instead of bluffing weakly? But how could he know for sure?

He heard a rattling sound from the booth. Let her get desperate; it gave him more of an edge. If only he could think what the hell to do with it.

Suddenly he heard a crashing sound. He wheeled around and ran back to the booth. The blow fell again, he saw the trapdoor shuddering. The crash again – she must be bracing herself against something and kicking with all of her might. Just his luck, she had to be a strong one.

He ran to the trapdoor just as the lock flew off. She pushed the door up – he kicked it down with all his weight, catching her hand as it tried to hold the door open. She screamed and pulled her hand back. He kicked the door again, savagely. He grabbed the metal cabinet and tipped it over against the trapdoor, jamming it in place. Gels and frames cascaded out of the cabinet, clattering onto the floor. The cabinet crashed into the door, biting a chink out of the wood. He shoved it in further, wedging it between the door and wire mesh of the cage, which bowed out from the strain of the upended corner.

He hung onto the tipped over cabinet, breathing heavily. Through the pounding in his ears he could hear her crying in there.

"Shut up, I'm trying to think!" he snapped. "I'm trying to think of a way to get out of this without killing you." He wiped some sweat from his eyes. "But I'm not coming up with anything."

SEVENTEEN

They walked up to the house that wasn't Jesse's and rang the bell until they were sure nobody was home.

Frank didn't say a word as they walked back to the rental car. They'd taken Carl's loaner because Frank's car had been stolen a few weeks ago. One-armed guys have all the luck.

Frank slipped into the passenger seat and looked over at Carl. "Not here," he said, "and not at your house. Now I'm going to have to ask you all the questions I didn't ask you before, because I was afraid if I thought about it too much I'd wake up and you'd disappear. Are you under psychiatric care? Are you a sadist? Are you prone to hallucinations? Are you a hallucination?"

Carl could tell that Frank was half-joking, so he half-laughed. "No, no, no, and no." *But why should he take your word for it*, Carl wondered. "I think we better call the police."

Frank sighed, "I want this to be true more than anything in the world and I just barely believe you. What makes you think the police will?"

"We can try."

"It would be so much better if we found her ourselves."

"I don't understand why she didn't come back here. She finds herself in a car with a strange man. She must have been scared."

"No, she wasn't," Frank said, quietly.

"What do you mean?"

"She was scared at first. But five or six blocks along, she forgot all about the strange man. All she'd know is, she's driving a car she doesn't know and she's going somewhere."

"Where?"

"What time was this?"

"Yesterday afternoon, around one."

"Just in time for fifth period."

Carl started the car and drove to the school.

Ryan was on his last cigarette when he realized that he couldn't hurt her. It had been worse than pointless to threaten her. He rolled over on the couch and reached for the beer on his desk. Every ten minutes or so he'd hear her start up again – he could hear it all the way in the office now that he was listening for it. The kicking at the trap door, the calling out 'Is anyone there?' She always sounded just as hopeful that there'd be an answer. Ryan was a little hurt that she seemed so sure he'd gone. He'd known his threat was empty, but it injured his pride to know it was so obvious to her.

But she wasn't just an ordinary girl, he knew that by now. Any ordinary person would have assumed he meant what he said. This was the only safe way to act. But this girl knew he was bluffing. She must have heard threats before, learned how to tell the dangerous from the ridiculous. No, this wasn't the first scrape she'd been in. She was too strong, she knew how to handle herself too well. He had to admire her in spite of his own situation. Here he was, holding all the cards, keeping her trapped in the dark, and yet she still had him on the defensive.

"And it's all because she thinks she knows me. She knows that I'll never hurt her, that I'll have to let her out, or at least leave her alone to let someone else find her. And she's right; she's read me like a book, even though she's never seen me."

But no, he corrected himself, "I'm the one who hasn't seen her." She'd seen him, that was the whole problem. But he couldn't give up, not while he still had her here. A girl like that, who's seen rough times, there must be some way around her. She could play at moral indignation all she wanted, but he knew she was only doing this for the fun of it, for the kick of having power and using it. Maybe he could find something else she wanted.

He climbed off the sofa and walked back onto the stage. He kept it dark back there. No one was around, but there was no need to attract unnecessary attention. He opened the loading dock door and looked out at the parking lot. There were a dozen or so cars in there now. There were always people in the school, even on the weekend, but they'd have no reason to come to the auditorium. He knew it was safe here, safe until Tuesday if he needed it. But keeping her here wouldn't help. So what if he starved a promise out of her? He'd have to let her out in the end and what possible reason would she have to keep her word?

A Chrysler New Yorker pulled into the parking lot and two men climbed out – the shorter of the two had only one arm. Ryan swiftly shut the door and darted backstage.

The metal cabinet was still tilted over and wedged between the wire of the cage and the trapdoor. It was all perfectly quiet. He'd have to talk to her now. But it would have to be very different. He couldn't threaten her; she was too strong for that. Even buying her off would have to be done with respect. Whatever he did he couldn't talk to her through the door anymore. If he wanted her on his side, he'd have to talk to her face to face.

"Jessica?" He did his best to sound avuncular through the plywood. There was no answer. So maybe she was asleep in there, or maybe she was crawling up there like a rat in the ceiling trying to find another way out. Or maybe she was waiting in there quietly to run as soon as he opened the door. That was the one thing he couldn't afford. To have her run out before he'd had the chance to say his piece; to have her run straight to the police with her bruised hand and say 'Mr. Ryan locked me up after I caught him fucking a fourteen year old girl.'

Ryan winced at the imagined accusation. The funny thing was that word for word it was all true. Wasn't it odd how the stating of bald facts could make anything, even something he knew to be perfectly human and understandable, sound positively evil? It was enough to make you lose your faith in the truth.

He whispered to the door again, "Jessica? Now I'm sorry about before, but I got a little panicky and you can't blame me for that. Now I'm going to open the door and let you out and you can go, or do whatever you want, but I want to talk to you first, okay?"

No answer.

"Bitch," he murmured under his breath. She wasn't going to make this easy for him. Well, there was no point in cursing her, he told himself. Sometimes you just have to play politics. He shifted the cabinet so he could open the door. This took some work. He couldn't stand it upright again; the best he could do was push it aside so that it was wedged against the wall next to the trapdoor and even that took a lot of grunting and groaning.

When he was done he sat down to catch his breath and watched the door, waiting for it to fly open and wondering what he'd do if he saw her run past him. Wish her luck, he supposed, and hope she gave him enough time to drive to Mexico.

The door didn't open. He reached out and pulled it open himself. There was no one there, but that didn't surprise him now. Actually he felt relieved. If she was up there she couldn't run out on him. If he could find her in there they'd have a chance to talk. Everything was riding on that talk and he realized with a blush that he had no idea what he was going to say to her. He told himself to trust to his famous talent for persuasion. After all, it had gotten him this far.

He grabbed a flashlight from the top of the light board and started to climb into the wall. Then something made him turn quickly so that he dropped the trapdoor on his leg with a crack.

Someone was knocking on the loading dock door.

EIGHTEEN

Carl knocked on the loading dock doors, hearing them echo, knowing no one would answer.

When he had seen his car, silver and stately in the afternoon light, he had run to it as if it were an old friend. He half expected to see her curled up in the back seat, asleep. But she wasn't there, and no unlikely clue as to her whereabouts was produced by his unreasonably hopeful search of the interior.

The car had been his only link to her and now that she was separated from it, she seemed more lost to him than ever. He walked with Frank to the school and went from door to door, finding no one, Frank averting his eyes from Carl's face.

They were turning from the loading dock door now, and Frank was about to say something, when the door opened. A short, stocky man with curly red hair and a neatly trimmed beard looked out at them.

"Yeah?" he asked.

"Hello, I was wondering if you saw a woman here yesterday. In her late twenties, a white dress, long sandy colored hair?"

"Here?" He shrugged. His face was expressive in a European way and his eyes frank and blue and easy to trust. Carl liked him immediately. "Just the kids and the teachers. Is something wrong?"

"No, but..." Hell, was there really any reason not to tell him? He found an old business card the studio had printed for him in his wallet and handed it over – it was the first time he could remember giving one out. "Here's my name and number. If you see her, give me a call. You see, she's a little disoriented." He tapped his forehead with two fingers.

Frank was next to him now, smiling and cutting him off. "But, I think we've taken up enough of your time. Thank you."

The man was still reading the scrap of paper. He looked up and smiled happily. "I'll call if I see anything," he said and Carl's heart sank a little as he went back in and shut the door on them.

Carl turned to him in irritation. "How am I supposed to find something out if you don't let me talk?"

Carl was amazed at how clearly the hurt registered on Frank's face. "I'm sorry, Carl."

Carl sat down on the edge of the loading dock, letting his legs dangle despondently. Frank stood next to him and cleared his throat in embarrassment. "This is true, isn't it, Carl?"

There was no humor in his question this time, but no anger either. For the first time Carl realized how crazy it was. Not the story, not Jesse's reappearance, but how easily Frank had believed him. A stranger comes to him with this tale and no proof and off he goes looking for her. He must love her very much, Carl thought with an acute feeling of uneasiness. He reached into his pocket for some bit of proof to offer as comfort to this rival. He pulled out the car keys he'd found in the greenhouse. "Here are her keys."

Frank took them from Carl's hand, glanced over them and tossed them back to Carl. "They're not hers."

"Well, she had them."

"What are you going to do if we find her?"

"Take her back to the house, feed her, keep her warm."

"Then what?"

"Take her back to her husband."

Frank just sat in silence for a moment. "I don't know about that..."

Carl looked up at Frank. "You think I'm right about him?"

Frank was quiet for a moment. "I wouldn't want to bet her life on it," he finally said.

The silence that hung between them was broken by a high-pitched chirping sound coming from the parking lot. It sounded like a single cry from a jungle bird, but it was the sound of a remote controlled lock on a car door. Carl looked at the keys in his hand. He'd been fumbling with them idly, pressing the button on the key chain. He pressed it again. Another chirp.

They leapt from the loading dock and Carl kept pressing the button while they followed the chirping sound, like children playing a game of 'warmer-colder.' Together, they zeroed in on a large black Mercedes. Carl pressed his key again and they watched through the window as the lock shot up and down.

———

The first thing he noticed when he flung open the trapdoor was a stinging, acrid scent. He focused his light on a pool of vomit. She was sleeping away from it, curled up like a child.

So he whispered, "Jessica?" his voice full of calmness and fatherly assurance.

She shifted a bit, mumbling to herself. Then she began to roll over and stretch. She sat up, her face still in shadow. "Who's that?" she asked.

"It's me, Ted. I'm a friend of Carl's."

He shifted the beam of light and he saw her face for the first time. There was not a trace of fine pubescent fat on that face. It was a face run through with lines of age. A woman's face.

Ryan simply stared. The wonderful thought that had come to him on the loading dock, the wonderful thought that he'd barely let himself believe, was coming true.

"Jessica? How old are you, Jessica?"

"Eighteen."

"And you know somebody named Carl Robson, don't you?"

"Is he here?"

He felt such a joy, such a total relief that he couldn't help but laugh, echoing loudly throughout the theater. He saw again in his mind Carl's simple little two-fingered gesture to his forehead, a gesture that was his salvation. Crazy, he thought, the woman is crazy. He was giddy. It was like he'd been in the gas chamber, the whole world staring at him with hate filled eyes and suddenly discovered it was all a dream. He wanted to kiss his pillow in gratitude.

Found out at last, but the woman is crazy, so it's like it never happened.

"Eighteen is a wonderful age, Jessica," he said, still laughing.

NINETEEN

Getting her out to the car wasn't too difficult. He just said he'd take her to Carl and, at the time, that was what he meant to do. But as he pulled out of the long school driveway onto Glenoaks the high of his relief began to evaporate and was replaced by a feeling of something unfinished, nagging at him like a post-coital depression.

Jenny. He had to tell her there was nothing to worry about now. And he had to tell her before her behavior made it obvious to everyone that there <u>was</u> something to worry about.

The best way to set her mind at ease was to introduce her to the crazy chick in the passenger seat he thought, glancing over at her. The crazy chick was wearing a backless sundress. He guessed it had started out white, but now it was covered with grime and dust and so was her skin. Her hair was plastered to the side of her face with sweat. She glanced back at him self-consciously and tried to brush it away with her scratched and bruised hand. The gesture was touching; the pathetic attempt of an insane, filthy wretch to improve her appearance. That was the first feeling of affection he'd had for her.

"We're going to go somewhere else first. I want you to meet a friend of mine, then I'll take you home, okay?"

She nodded and smiled shyly. A lost lamb, he thought, and aren't we all?

———

As soon as he saw Jenny's mother 's face he knew he was too late. She stammered something about Jenny not feeling well and not wanting to be disturbed. He smiled calmly and told her it would keep.

He kept the panic out of his steps as he walked back to his car, feeling on the skin of his back that the front door was still open, that she was still staring at him as he moved. And maybe Jenny was too, from one of the windows. Hiding ashamed behind a curtain, watching the man she'd betrayed.

Jessica was still sitting in the passenger seat, looking out at him with politely concealed boredom. Then a startled look came into her eyes. Ryan had just a second to think she was lapsing into some kind of manic-depressive hysteria before he heard Jenny's mother yelling "NO!" and feet clumping across the lawn behind him. Heavy, masculine feet. Should he run? An innocent man would just turn. He just turned.

Before his turn was complete, a rough hand grabbed his shoulder and shoved him against the car.

"I ought to fucking kill you, you know that? I ought to fucking smash your head in!"

"What's the matter?" Ryan asked, all shock and concern.

"You know what the fuck's the matter!"

"I'm sorry?" he replied, vaguely aware that he was stealing his blank replies from his conversations with Jessica.

"I'm gonna have your fucking job, and I hope they send you to prison and somebody knifes you in the goddamned shower."

"I'm sorry, but I really don't know what you're talking about."

Jenny's father yanked him up by the shoulders. "I know what you did to my daughter."

Easy enough to reply. Easy enough to spit in his face and let him take him apart. There isn't much point in lying. Ryan was done for and he knew it. But he lied anyway, just on principle.

"Jenny's a troubled girl, Mr. Kallen," he made a casual gesture with his right hand. "I've been trying…"

The casual gesture was a mistake. Kallen slapped his hand down and it cracked against the window.

"Don't try any shit with me, or I'll fucking kill you right now."

Jenny's mother called out something restraining from the porch and Ryan took advantage of the distraction to open his car door.

"Maybe we'd better talk this over when you've calmed down."

Kallen shoved the door so that it pressed hard against Ryan's chest. "When I calm down I'm gonna call your wife, then I'm gonna call the principal, then I'm gonna call the goddamn cops."

"Okay, you do what you think is best, but I think you also ought to consider what's best for Jenny."

Dangerous, he told himself as he felt Kallen shove the door harder, pressing it into his ribs. All Kallen said was "Jenny" but it burst out of him like a curse stronger than Ryan had ever heard.

But the wife was back there again, begging him off. Bless her, Ryan thought. Kallen stepped back and Ryan slipped into the car.

He could have pulled out right then. Instead he kept talking through the half opened door. "Haven't you noticed she's been acting strangely, Mr. Kallen? I hate to use the word drugs, Mr. Kallen, but…"

Kallen slammed the door shut and began kicking the side of the car so hard Ryan could almost see the dents. He started the car and peeled out, leaving Kallen running after him half a block swearing and shaking his fists like a child in a tantrum. Then he saw him run back into his house.

Ryan figured it would take about five minutes to drive home. Time for Kallen to make how many calls? And who would he call first? The trick was to keep acting innocent. What would he do if he were innocent?

"Are you okay?"

He'd forgotten she was there and hearing her voice like that he almost jumped out the window.

"Yeah, I'm fine, he's crazy. The world's full of crazy people."

She laughed. "You said it."

You should know, he said to himself, laughing at her laugh. "Look, I gotta go somewhere right away, it's very important. Then I'll take you home okay?"

"Thanks. What's your name?"

He looked at her in surprise. "I told you five minutes ago, did you forget already?"

She looked suddenly defensive. "You didn't tell me. You didn't tell me."

"You forgot already? How often do you forget things?"

"I don't forget things. What are you talking about?"

"Where'd we meet?"

A pause. "What difference does it make?" She sounded petulant now.

"Come on, we were just there ten minutes ago. Where'd we meet?"

"I don't know, I don't remember, who cares?" She curled up by the door on her side and stared at the floor of the car, wounded.

Jesus Christ, he thought, she forgets everything as soon as it happens. What an annoying disease.

Why couldn't everyone have it?

TWENTY

He drove Jessica to the grocery store on Glendale, gave her money for a cab and told her to find her own way home. She thanked him. He told her to forget about it and he didn't think that would be too difficult for her.

When he pulled out he saw Ernie, the old black man who washed cars in the parking lot for spare change. Ernie smiled and waved. Ryan waved back and cursed to himself. But he shook it off. So he dropped someone off at the store? There was no reason for anyone to connect her with the alleged events in the school auditorium. And even if someone did, and even if that someone got hold of Jessica, it wouldn't matter. Jessica wouldn't tell them a thing. Jessica was someone he could trust.

Still, what if they ask the simple question, 'who was that woman?' He'd have to come up with an answer. There were a lot of things he'd have to come up with. He checked his watch and wondered if he could still get home before Kallen called.

———

"You're looking beautiful today, dear."

"Fuck off and die you son of a bitch."

He guessed that Kallen had called.

"I knew you were fucking somebody, but a fourteen year old girl? I knew you were fucking somebody, but I didn't know you were sick."

"The man's upset, I don't blame him. His daughter's very disturbed, she has a crush on me, now she's started making up these stories."

"Don't, just don't. You can lie to everybody, but not to me. I know you, that's the sad thing, I know you."

"You want to believe this, don't you? You want to believe the worst of me."

"There's no best of you."

"I love this. I'm the teacher, I'm the adult, and I don't get the benefit of the doubt over some drugged up teen-ager – Where are you going?"

"I'm leaving. I'd throw <u>you</u> out, but the house is too cheap to fight over."

"So it all comes down to money, is that it?"

"Good God, can't you show a little courage once and tell the truth?"

But she's wrong, it would be easy to tell the truth. It's lying when everyone knows the truth that takes courage."

"This girl's trying to destroy me. I need you to stand by me."

"I hope they send you to prison and some big drug dealer makes you his boy toy."

Funny how that's everyone's idea of the nightmare of prison now, Ryan reflected. It used to be the loss of freedom, the stripping away of one's free will, the four gray walls, the forced separation from nature and one's family and friends. Now it's unwelcome intercourse with a large, rude man. Just another aspect of our society's unhealthy obsession with sex.

"How can you joke about this?" he asked.

"You think this is a little game, a little adventure? Fucking a child will make you young again?"

"She's not a child!" *Wrong thing to say,* Ryan told himself, *make a note never to say that again.*

"Well, at least after you she has nowhere to go but up."

With that, his wife was gone.

Getting her back again was going to be a little harder this time.

But okay, how bad is that? If she could get over the bitterness and pain it might be a chance to start over.

And there was nothing she could really say to hurt him legally, was there? He knew they couldn't make a wife testify against her husband, but he wasn't so sure if they could stop one from doing it.

He went to the bedroom and got out some of the stuff he had shoved into the back of his sock drawer. Then he got in his car and drove to the school.

He noticed that there was still dust from Jessica's dress on the passenger seat and brushed it off at a red light. But the dust was still on her dress. If the police check it will they know where it came from?

But why would the police check it? They wouldn't be looking for her. They wouldn't be looking for anyone. Because there wasn't any third person up there in the ceiling. Jenny was the one who was up there, wasn't she? That was where Ryan found her. And he was very shocked and she started making threats.

He checked his watch. It was about fifteen minutes since Kallen must have called his wife. So he's talked to Presser by now, but Presser wouldn't call the police right away. He'd want to talk to Ryan first before getting one of his best teachers in serious trouble.

So Presser was probably calling him right now. And there was no one home, but there's nothing suspicious about that. I'll call him as soon as I get home, Ryan thought.

He went into the school parking lot and parked in back behind the gym. He knew the door would be open there on account of basketball practice. It wasn't too hard to get in without being seen, not that that really mattered. Hell, he had a right to be there, didn't he?

Jenny's locker was by the clinic. He remembered where it was because he used to hang out there and chat with her between classes. Was anybody's affection ever so misguided?

Those combination locks couldn't be easier to crack, you could hear the tumblers from across the hall. He opened it, put half a gram of cocaine, a plastic film container of pot and a bag of Quaaludes on the top shelf, behind her geography book. He closed it up, spun the dial and went on to the auditorium.

When he went into the light booth he straightened up the shelf again and set all the gels back on it, neatly. He took some tools out of the storage room and used a chisel on the broken lock, chipping it off from the outside. Then he went into the tunnel, rolled two joints, smoked half of one, put it out and let the other one burn. He left the pool of vomit, thinking it gave the whole mise-en-scene a touch of authenticity.

He went out the same way he came in and again no one saw him. He drove home, resisting the temptation to speed. After the misunderstanding with his wife, he'd gone out for a drive, just to let off some steam, had a burger at Tony's – no, at In 'n' Out, no one expected anybody to remember you there.

Not that anybody would be checking. He thought he'd taken care of everything fairly well. It would be his word against Jenny's and who were they going to believe, a respected teacher or some teen-ager hiding in the walls, smoking pot and vomiting her lungs out?

Of course she'd say it hadn't been her vomiting, it had been this 'other girl.' That was the wonderful thing about her story – this phantom girl in the ceiling, the very part of it that had caused the whole problem, would sound like the lie. Something of child would make up to dodge punishment. "It wasn't me, really it wasn't, it was this 'other girl.'" How pathetic.

There was a Beatles song on the radio and he sang along. When he got two yards from his house he slammed on the brakes.

Jessica was on the front step.

TWENTY-ONE

Carl sat down on his driveway, leaning back against the hubcap of the black Mercedes. Frank was still in the passenger seat, digging through the glove compartment for the third time. No sign of Jesse. No trace of the owner.

Frank slammed the glove compartment shut and swore. "Damn it, no registration, no nothing."

"It doesn't make sense." Carl had said all this before. "If she'd just taken off with the car, like she did with mine, all that stuff would be in there. Unless the car was already stolen? Or somebody just gave it to her, but didn't want it to be traced?"

"Is that what doesn't make sense to you?" Frank asked, "Is that the part that doesn't make sense?" He got up out of the car and walked into the house.

Carl had reclaimed his car from the high school parking lot and driven it home, and Frank had insisted on taking the Mercedes himself. He'd followed Carl to the house, full of enthusiasm, sure that a thorough search of the car was bound to turn up the vital clue that would prove Jesse was still alive and tell them where she'd gone. Instead, nothing. Nothing but Carl's story.

When Carl came in he found Frank at the kitchen table, nursing a cup of coffee.

"I'm not making this up," was all Carl could think of to say.

"Of course not, you've probably got a tumor of your own."

Carl sat down across from him. "I know there's no reason in the world for you to believe me…"

"There's no reason for me not to." Frank set the cup down and looked out the window. "Martin is always telling me to put all of this behind me, to get on with my life. But the thing is, before Jesse, I never really had a life. I had a routine. I did things. But aside from the accident," he gestured with his prosthetic arm, "nothing ever happened to me. But she happened. And it was like a train wreck. It was big and painful and beautiful and <u>every second</u> mattered. You know what Beaudelaire said about love? It's 'an oasis of horror in a desert of boredom.' But it's still an oasis. Our time together, that's the story of my life. Everything before her was just the boring set up. Like the first hour of a mini-series, the part that's just padding to stretch it out for three nights. And the time since she's gone, that's just been some sort of weird, dragged out anti-climax. I can feel myself sitting in the audience watching my life and wondering, 'why isn't this movie over?'" He laughed and sipped his coffee. "So, if this is just some psychosis of yours, or some bizarre con game, it really doesn't matter to me, at least it's a part of my story." He shoved the coffee cup aside and looked intently at Carl. "So what else have you got?"

Carl felt suddenly on the spot, like a third grader called on by his teacher unexpectedly. "How about Jeff?"

Frank looked up sharply. "What about him?"

He told Frank about Jeffrey's letter and how Martin had claimed he'd visited the week before her death.

Frank grunted thoughtfully and Carl asked him what was wrong.

"Well, that's not true," Frank said. "I was practically living in the house then, I would have known. Jeff hasn't been back for over a year."

"Why would Martin lie about that?"

"I don't know." Frank was hunched forward now. "He hasn't been able to find Jeff yet, right?"

"That's what he told me."

"Are you sure Jeff wrote the letter?"

Carl coughed. "You think Martin forged the letter?"

"I don't know."

"But why? So we'd think Jeff visited when he didn't? What would that get him?"

"I don't know. You're right, never mind."

"If you could see that letter," Carl said, "would you at least know if Jeffrey wrote it?"

"I suppose, but what's the point?"

"Let's look at it from another angle. Maybe the letter isn't supposed to convince us that he came, maybe it's supposed to convince us that he left."

"But if he never came, who'd care if he left?"

"Frank, that letter is the only reason everybody thinks Jeff is still in Peru. And because they think he's off, running around in the jungle or the rain forest or whatever they have down there, no one thinks it's strange that he can't be found. But what if he's not there. What if <u>that's</u> what Martin is covering up?"

Frank stared at him in disbelief. "You think Martin did something to Jeffrey?"

"I didn't say that."

"What then? Jeffrey's the one that killed her? Oh that's right, nobody killed her, she's still running around out there." He stood up, quickly, his chair skidding on the floor. "Why the fuck am I sitting here listening to this? I'm getting to be as crazy as everybody thinks I am."

Frank made his way to the door and as he passed the phone, it rang. He picked it up automatically, not thinking, because that's what you do with a ringing phone. When he put the receiver to his ear, the blood drained from his face.

Then he was croaking, "What? Hello?" and hammering on the lever, trying to preserve a lost connection. Carl didn't even remember moving to his side.

"What is it?" Carl asked.

"She got cut off," Frank said.

"Who?"

"Jesse," he said, very quietly.

TWENTY-TWO

Bad penny, Ryan thought as he pulled into his driveway. She keeps turning up like a bad penny.

She had a bag of groceries in her arms and she craned her neck to look at him as he climbed out of the car. She didn't seem at all satisfied by what she saw.

Ernie the car wash man came from around the side of the house and smiled at him warmly.

"Hey, Mr. Ryan, you know this girl?"

"No, I don't Ernie."

He shook his head in disappointment. "Damn," he said, "Damn, damn."

"That's what I told you," Jesse said. "I don't know why nobody listens to me." She sat down on the curb looking quite forlorn. "I wish somebody knew what was going on."

"What is this, Ernie?"

"I'm sorry Mr. Ryan, but I thought I saw you drop this girl off in the Von's parking lot. Didn't I see you, didn't I wave to you?"

"You did Ernie, but…"

"But you don't know her?"

This was the curse of friendliness, thought Ryan. Here was a man he'd made the mistake of smiling at, or giving a little business to out of charity – as if a man couldn't wash his own car – a man he'd chatted with to show that he had no sense of class or race superiority. And it all came around now to bite him in the butt.

"Well…" he began.

Fortunately, Ernie wanted to tell his story.

"'Cause I saw her wandering around the parking lot like she didn't know where she was and didn't know what she was supposed to do and I knew the look 'cause I got a brother who's a retard and he always got this look on his face like he don't know where the hell he is. Then she goes into the store and after a while comes out with these groceries and starts wandering around the parking lot like she's looking for her car. Well, I know she ain't got a car, 'cause I saw you drop her off, or someone who looks like you just when you were there. Anyway I figure it looks like it might rain anyway so nobody's gonna want a wash so I go up to her and ask her what's wrong. She says she thinks somebody stole her car, but I can tell she's not really sure herself. I figure she must belong somewhere so I offer to take her home and she isn't sure at first if maybe she should call the police instead, but she says since she can't really remember where she parked her car anyway she might just look stupid. So she says okay."

"So we get in my old car and I drive her home but she don't even really know where she's going 'cause when we get to her house she says that's not it, somebody took it and she's real upset. You know, life's not so easy for people with all their brains but for retards it's a real bitch of a place, and I think an intellectual guy like you can appreciate that, right Mr. Ryan?"

"Yes, you're very enlightened Ernie." Ryan was quite irritated by the fact that Ernie had a car of his own. He'd always assumed Ernie was an impoverished, homeless person. What was the point of being charitable to someone who wasn't impoverished or homeless?

"Thank you, thanks a lot. That means a lot coming from you. Anyway, I'm starting to wonder what the hell I should do with her when I remember that you dropped her off, or it looked like you did and I figured I'd bring her here and maybe you'd know where she belonged."

"How'd you know where I live, Ernie?"

"I looked you up in the phone book Mr. Ryan. I ain't the retard."

"Of course not, Ernie."

"But if you're not the one, I guess I'll…" he looked over at her with a frustrated sigh. She rooted through her groceries, pulled out an apple and started eating it. "Look at her, she's just like a kid. I mean I'd just think she was one of those fucking street nuts but I thought I saw somebody drop her off and hell, she had money for groceries. I guess I better call the cops. Not that they'll do anything…"

"Don't do that, Ernie."

"Why not, Mr. Ryan?"

"Well, to be honest Ernie, and this is a little embarrassing, I do know her."

He looked at him with blank surprise. "You do?"

"Yes. I – I've been having a little trouble with the wife," Ryan never said things like 'the wife,' but this seemed the proper time to begin, "she gets jealous over the littlest thing. And so when I found this lady…she was hitchhiking on an off ramp and she didn't know where she was going so I loaned her a little money and dropped her off. I figured she'd call a cab or something, I didn't realize she was…disabled. The only reason I denied it was, well, I didn't want my wife to misunderstand."

"Oh, I see. So why can't I call the police?"

"Well, that might be something of a shock, don't you think? I mean, look at her." She was sitting on the steps, munching the apple and giving them bored, dirty looks. "She's never had anything to do with the police. Why don't you let me look after her?"

"Oh, I couldn't do that, Mr. Ryan."

"Why not?"

"I don't want you to get in trouble with the old lady."

"I'm willing to take that risk, Ernie."

"Aw, but this isn't fair to you. Let me worry about it, I didn't mean to dump trouble on you."

The hell you didn't. "It's no trouble, Ernie. In a way I feel responsible."

"Why?"

"I just do. Why don't you go home and I'll take care of this."

"Hey, I got an idea. I'll just drop her off at the Galleria. She can be somebody else's problem."

"I don't think that would be right, do you? Don't you think we all have a moral responsibility to each other as human beings?"

"Well yeah, but not when it's this much trouble."

"Let me take care of it, Ernie."

"And your wife, what's your wife going to say?"

"My wife's out of town."

"Then what were you worried about her for?"

"I'm an idiot, Ernie."

"No you're not Mr. Ryan."

"Thank you, Ernie. I really want to do this."

"Well, okay."

He turned to go back to his car. Ryan hustled up to him and spoke to him very quietly. "But if anybody asks you, this didn't happen, okay?"

Ernie stared at him blankly. "Why not?"

Unbelievable, Ryan thought. "The wife," he said with a patient smile.

"Oh right. You're not gonna try anything with her, are you?"

Ryan looked stunned. "What?"

"Well, I don't really know you that well, do I Mr. Ryan?"

Then what the fuck are you doing here? he wanted to scream. "Trust me. She'll be perfectly safe. I remember she had a phone number with her. I'll call it, somebody'll come pick her up, everything'll be fine."

"I could do that."

"Please let me. You see, I felt very guilty about dropping her off like that. This'll let me make up for it."

Ernie looked at him. "Oh, I see."

"Good, so why don't you go now?"

"Okay." Ernie walked over to Jesse who had just finished her apple and was smoothing out her dress, trying to wipe the dirt off it. "Jessica, I'm leaving you here with Mr. Ryan, is that okay?"

"Who is he?"

Ernie looked up at Ryan, surprised. "She doesn't know you."

"Come on, Jessie, I'm Ted Ryan. I'm Carl's friend, I'm going to take you to Carl, remember?"

She was standing now, relieved and smiling. "You know Carl?"

"Sure I do. And his friend, the one armed guy, what's his name?" Mistake, Ryan thought when he saw the puzzled look come back to her face. Cover, move back. "Carl Rooney, right? I have his number. You wait here, I'll give him a call, he'll come get you, okay?"

She looked from him to Ernie once, then said, "Okay."

Ernie smiled. "Good. Bye, Jesse honey, take care of yourself. You give me a call Ryan, let me know how it all turned out."

Ryan smiled and said, "Right." *Right I'll call you, you bastard and see if I ever let you wash my fucking car again.*

He took Jesse's arm and led her up to the door. "Come on Jesse, let's wait inside, it's cooler."

Inside, he shut the door quickly and watched Ernie's old wreck lumber out and head down the street.

"Who is that guy," Jesse said. "Do you know that guy, is he crazy?"

Ryan took Jesse's arm again and led her to the bedroom. He pulled a pair of jeans and a t-shirt from his wife's drawer and threw them on the bed.

"Change into these," he said.

"Why?" She was scared now, damn it. It would be easier if she wasn't scared, but he didn't have the energy to reassure her.

"Cause you look like hell."

She looked down at her dress, feeling a little ashamed. That was better.

"I don't even know this dress."

"Good, then you won't mind me burning it."

Now, you said that deliberately to scare her, Ryan thought. Does it really make a difference?

"Burn it?"

The dress had to be burned, he thought, just in case they did try to check that dust. And she had to be far away. He'd load her in the car and drive for an hour, drop her off in Long Beach or somewhere where no one could make a connection.

"It's a joke, don't you like jokes?"

She sat down on the bed, running a hang through her greasy hair.

"Christ, is everybody crazy?"

"Not everybody."

She stared back at him and he didn't even think of looking away. "I want to go home."

He picked up the clothes again and tossed them at her. "Put these on."

She caught them and threw them back in his face. "No."

Ryan shoved her back onto the bed and climbed on top of her, cupping his hand under her chin. "Listen bitch, you don't have a home. I killed your family and burned down your house and if you don't change like I say, I'll get you too."

She laughed again. "You're crazy."

He let her sit up. "I don't think so. I think you're the crazy one. You're the one who can't remember anything, where you got your dress, who I am, where your house went. You don't even know you're a mental case." He grabbed one of his wife's old fashioned hand mirrors off the bed table. "How old are you?"

"Seventeen. I'm getting out of here."

He grabbed her arm and held her. "You're seventeen? Take a look." He held the mirror up to her face.

She didn't react at first, then suddenly the mirror was cracking against his forehead, her hands were slapping at his face and her legs were kicking at his knees. He fell to the floor, swinging his arms wildly to keep her off him.

He tried to crawl under the bed, but the feet kept kicking at him and then the mirror started pounding on his back, the edge digging into his ribs. He tried to turn over so it wouldn't keep hitting the same place. A foot came up to kick him again and he grabbed it and bit at the ankle, tasting blood.

The mirror came down on the back of his head. He heard glass breaking. He reached up and grabbed a hand – he hoped it was the one he'd caught in the trapdoor. He pulled on it as hard as he could, slamming it into the sharp corner of the bed table.

He shifted around so he could move his other arm and swung it up with all his strength into some part of her that was soft and she backed off, gasping for air. He pulled himself up onto his feet, blinking his right eye to keep the blood out of it.

He reached up to wipe it off and she was on him again, clambering on top of him, forcing him to the floor on his knees. He reached up and started yanking on her hair.

He threw himself to the floor and she toppled off him. He clambered to his knees, found her face and started hitting it with the sides of his hands till she stopped yelling and didn't look like she wanted to get up anymore.

Grabbing onto the blankets, he pulled himself to his feet and kicked her. He saw that she was trying to crawl under the bed just like he'd been doing before. He decided to stop.

He sat on the bed for a moment, listening to her crying under the bed. He remembered the blood in his eye again and went into the bathroom. Pray God she hadn't done any damage to his face, anything he'd have to explain.

There was a small cut on his forehead and it was bleeding like the dickens. It would stop soon though, and he could comb his hair down to cover it. Other than that he looked fine. There were aches all over his body, so he took his shirt off and there he hadn't fared so well. There was one big welt on his back. Tomorrow he'd be covered with bruises. He pulled off his trousers – there was a gash on one ankle. He didn't even remember how that had happened, but it was already starting to clot.

He put his clothes back on and went into the bedroom. He pulled her out from under the bed. She didn't resist much, she was crying too hard. She was going to look a lot worse than he was. There was a black eye already starting and he could see where a clump of her hair was gone. There was a bite mark on her ankle, but he thought that only made them even. He started taking her dress off.

She resisted at first, but so half-heartedly, it was almost funny. "Don't worry," he said, "you're not my type." He kept talking as he pulled the dress over her head, just to pass the time. "But I could, you know. Nobody would know. You wouldn't even know, because you're too fucking crazy. Did you know that? It's the old philosophical question, if you fuck a tree in the forest and no one hears it, does it make a sin?"

The phone rang. He started to answer it there but he figured it would be better to take it in another room. When he locked the bedroom door he could just see her half-naked, crawling back under the bed.

He dumped the dress in the kitchen trash can and picked up the phone.

Presser was on the other end. "Ted, this is Dennis. Look, this is difficult..."

"I know what it's about, Dennis. I talked to Mr. Kallen, he called my wife..."

"Well, Ted I know this is difficult, but we really have to check these things out."

"Dennis, I understand, you got your job to do. Besides, this is a serious matter and it really has to be looked into."

"That's right."

"I mean," Ryan went on, sympathetically, "we all suspected this girl had problems, but I don't think any of us guessed how serious they were until today." He reached over and flicked a switch to start the coffee brewing.

"Well, yeah, Ted, her parents are very upset," Presser said, not giving anything away.

"Of course they are and how can you blame them? They love her, naturally they'd believe her. I'm surprised that she'd exploit that, but to be fair to her, she's very confused."

"She seems confused."

"So you've talked to her?" Ryan asked.

"Well, we've spoken. I really tried to call you first, but you were out." Was that a slightly apologetic tone creeping into Presser's voice?

"Well, Gloria was very upset about this whole thing," Ryan explained. "She's going to visit her sister and, well, this'll sound silly but I went out for a burger and a shake."

"I understand."

"I don't have to tell you there's no truth to any of this, do I, Denny?"

"Of course not, Ted, of course not. But you understand I have to check..."

"Hey, don't apologize, we all want to help this girl. She's one of my best students, I'm very fond of her. I guess that's why I let her get me into this mess. I never thought she'd follow through on that crazy threat, but I guess she was scared."

"Why don't you tell me your side of it, Ted?"

"What do you mean 'side'?" he allowed a little irritation to slip into his voice. "I'll tell you the <u>truth</u> if you want."

"That's what I meant, Ted. I'm sorry."

"Well, I went to my office to finish up a little paperwork and do a little maintenance on the lights in the auditorium, when I smelled what I thought was pot. I mean I'm thirty-six, I don't have to pretend I don't know what it smells like, do I?"

Presser laughed. That was good, thought Ted.

"And I couldn't tell where it was coming from until I heard something behind the wall." He noticed the coffee was ready so he poured himself a cup and drank it while he finished the story. He left out the part about the vomit; he thought that would be more impressive as a surprise.

"She started crying, she said if I told her parents she'd make up some crazy story about me attacking her. I didn't believe her, but I have to confess I wasn't going to tell anyone. She seemed like she needed a second chance. Now I guess it's too late for that."

There was silence on the other end and Ryan felt the coffee start to brew again in his stomach. "Jesus," Presser said finally, "She seems like such a nice girl."

"Of course she is Dennis, otherwise she wouldn't be so scared. I mean, you've met her father, haven't you?"

"Sure."

"How did he strike you?"

"Well, he's upset…"

"No, I mean in general. He didn't seem violent to you? He didn't seem to have a temper?"

"…You think he's abusive?"

"Hey, don't put words in my mouth. I just think she might be really scared about him finding out."

"Jesus Christ," Dennis sighed. "Sometimes I wish I'd stayed a teacher."

Ryan gave what he hoped was a wry chuckle. "That ain't always so easy either, Bud."

"I know Ted, I know. Look, I want to resolve this without any legal shit."

"I appreciate that. If you just let me talk to her,"

"Whoa, I don't think I can do that."

"Hey, don't give me that, we're human beings, can't we just sit down and talk like human beings? Let's forget the red tape and just cut through to where this girl is hurting."

"No, that is absolutely out of the question, absolutely, you understand that?"

Back off Ryan, he told himself. But it was good to ask; it sounded so sincere and even naïve. Also it gave that asshole Presser a place to put his foot and feel like the boss. A place that didn't matter.

"You think there's any evidence of this substance abuse in that tunnel?"

Great, he's saying 'substance abuse,' he's already applying the proper clichés. "I don't know Dennis, I wasn't thinking that way."

"It'll be easier if there is. Look, come by my office in a half hour, we'll clear this up."

"Thanks, Dennis."

"Sorry about all this."

Ryan accepted the apology.

———

When she woke up she couldn't remember what she'd been dreaming about. She couldn't even remember that she'd been asleep really, but you had to be, didn't you, if you woke up? Anyway, she went from dark to light, from nothing to something, so that must have been sleeping and this must be waking.

She was huddled half under a bed and there were tears on her face, but no reason to be crying. Must have been a really bad dream, she thought, glad that she couldn't remember it. She rarely had bad dreams.

She reached out to pull herself from under the bed and her hand surprised her by aching with pain. It felt for all the world like something had been dropped on it, but she couldn't remember that happening. And as she crawled out she felt the pain coming from everywhere. Her head, when she moved it, started whirling with a hard, metal tasting pain.

It must be a bad flu, she thought, finding pain even in her scalp. She'd had a flu like this before – just before the fever set in you felt for all the world like someone had been beating you with a rubber hose.

She kept thinking that until she came out into the light and saw the blood on her hand. She gasped in confusion, wiping at the blood to see where the cut was, but it wasn't really a cut, more like a long torn bruise. She tried to pull herself up with the bedspread and it wasn't until then that she realized she didn't know where she was and that she was almost naked.

She dropped back to the floor wishing she could remember her bad dream. She looked around the room, trying to find some clue that could tell her why she was here. It was an ordinary bedroom, a grown-up bedroom. There was a double bed with blue sheets that were tossed and tumbled. There was broken glass on the floor. Other than that there was nothing threatening about the place except for her being there in her bra and panties, beaten and bleeding and not knowing where she was.

She brushed the broken glass away and sat back against the bed table. Her body seemed wrong too, heavy and sagging. Her breasts were drooping, her stomach seemed distended and her thighs were bloated. Something awful had been done to her. She couldn't have been raped, could she? But how could she forget something like that? As easily as you could forget being beaten up.

She heard a door open and she flinched, not knowing where to run, not even knowing where the door was. But the man she saw ran to her and kneeled next to her.

"God, are you all right?"

His face was full of concern and his frank blue eyes were stricken with worry. She liked his face, even though she never liked red heads.

"I don't know," she said. "I woke up and…"

"You don't have to say it, I know. We have to get out of here fast."

He lifted her to her feet and she leaned on him gratefully, not even feeling self-conscious about her nakedness. He seemed a little embarrassed by it though, he kept his eyes turned away and she thought that was cute. He picked a t-shirt and a pair of jeans off the bed and handed them to her.

"Here, you better put these on."

He kept his eyes away when she dressed and she thought that was even cuter. She thought it was strange that she could be attracted to a man after what she'd gone through, but when she remembered she didn't know what she'd gone through, it didn't seem so strange after all.

He led her out into the living room. He said he thought they had time for a drink before they ran and took her into the kitchen. He got her a Coke that said 'classic' on the side. She laughed and said she thought it was good but didn't think it was a classic. Then she asked who they were running from.

"It," he said looking straight at her.

"What's it?"

"The evil monster who stole eighteen years from you and killed everyone you know."

It was only then that she noticed the cut on his forehead and realized he might have been the one who was hitting her. She must have gotten a funny expression on her face, because he started laughing then. It was a hearty, good-natured laugh and for a second she joined in. Then she bolted from the table and ran for the kitchen door. He was there first, blocking her way, still laughing.

"I'm sorry, I shouldn't have laughed. Bad taste, bad taste. It's the strain."

"What strain?"

"You know, coming home, finding all those dead bodies in the basement, you upstairs."

"Bodies?"

"Yeah, the cleaning lady and a couple of the neighbor kids. You were a lucky girl. Unless...You weren't the one who chopped them up, were you?"

"Did you call the police?"

"The phone's dead. Even the phone is dead," he said, doing his best Boris Karloff from his favorite movie, The Black Cat. "Finish your Coke, we have to run in case he comes back."

He opened the door and ushered her out to the garage. It smelled of oil and old paint. The car was oddly small and looked like the back end had been lopped off. He led her around to the passenger side and opened the door. He was still smiling at her.

She lunged at the door, knocking it against his side. She climbed onto the hood of the car, rolled over it and ran through the kitchen door, slamming it shut and locking it. She ran to the phone, picked it up and dialed 911.

The kitchen door swung open and he stood there, leaning on the door jam, smiling. "It's my house, I got a key, you know."

She threw the phone at him and ran but she didn't know where the front door was and she turned the wrong way and ended up in a little office without any exit. He was there again, blocking her way. She picked up a heavy paperweight and held it high.

"Come on Jesse, I'm just trying to take you home, I'm trying to take you to see Carl, don't you want to see Carl?"

She wavered. "How do you know Carl?"

"He's my best friend, he saved my life in 'Nam. Tell me where he lives, I'll drop you off."

"Fuck off."

"Okay, I'm off on the wrong foot. I'd wait fifteen minutes and start fresh but I got to be somewhere, so just put that down and come with me!"

"Do you think I'm stupid?"

She's not, he thought. He was the fool to try to play games with her. Look at her there, holding that weight in her hand, beaten but defiant, without a bit of fear in her. She even looked young. He felt a surge of respect for her and a sorrow that he wasn't going to get to know her better.

He was even going to miss her, he realized. He'd spent so much time with her today. He'd been totally involved with her for hours now and she'd been so many things to him. First a druggie teen-ager fucking with his brain, then a poor lunatic and now this woman standing in front of him like a warrior, bloodied but unbowed. How many love affairs had that much variety?

He reached into his pocket and pulled out the scrap of paper Carl had given him. He dialed the number off it and held the phone in her ear.

She watched him suspiciously, listening to the phone ring. Then a voice said 'hello' and she grabbed the receiver.

He figured he'd just let her talk, let them plan a place to meet and then take her there. But then he thought about Carl knowing his face, knowing he was at the school and that she must have been there too. So when she said, "Carl, is that you" he pulled the cord out of the wall and grabbed her, thinking he didn't know what – thinking he could force her into the car, drive her out to the freeway, leave her there and still make it to the school in time, even though he had no idea how you could drag someone out of a house and into a car if they didn't want to go.

He couldn't. Just when he thought he had her arms pinned, one snaked free and she slammed the receiver into his groin. He fell back, groaning. She rushed by him, but he only reached out his hand and it didn't do a thing to stop her.

He heard her running and tried to put the pain out of his mind as he struggled to his feet and limped into the kitchen. He'd left the keys on the table when he ran after her and they were gone now. He heard his car start and staggered to the garage just in time to see it peeling off down the street. He thought about running after her, but it still hurt when he moved, so instead he just walked into the garage, sat down and laughed.

He knew another man might have been angry or worried, but he was always able to see the humor in things. That was what gave him his healthy attitude towards life.

TWENTY-THREE

Mr. and Mrs. Fletcher were gone for the day, and their daughter was back from college watching the baby, so she was the one who answered the door this time.

At nineteen Lucy had been living on her own at the dorm for two years and she'd seen a lot so she wasn't as scared as she might have been before. But she was young enough not to be as careful as she would be later, so she didn't slam the door and lock it or even talk to the lady in the doorway. Instead she asked her in.

The lady didn't know if she wanted to come in at first. She seemed very confused and just wanted to know where her house was. But Lucy didn't blame her for being confused. Not when she'd been beaten up that badly.

She offered the lady coffee but she wanted a Coke. She got some Zephrin Chloride from the bathroom and cleaned the wound and got some ice to put on her eye. Then she asked if she should call the police.

"I really just want to go home," the lady said.

"What's the number, can I call?"

"It's supposed to be here. God, I'm so fucking confused," the lady looked up at her, embarrassed. "Sorry," she said.

"That's okay, just relax."

Then little Alex started crying upstairs – that loud kind of howling that sent chills through Lucy whenever she heard it. She ran up, as always expecting to be greeted by gushes of blood and a ghastly accident.

Alex was standing in his crib howling and pointing at Mr. Bear who had slipped through the bars and was on the floor. Neither of them appeared to be injured. Lucy sighed with relief and tossed the bear back in the crib, telling her brother that Mr. Bear was okay.

Alex kept crying. She picked him up and tried bouncing him a little on her hip. He kept howling and started tugging on her shirt trying to get at her breasts.

"Sorry Honey," she said, "Sister's not equipped. If you're hungry I'll get you a bottle."

"Can I hold him?"

She hadn't known the lady had followed her up, but she was glad for the help and she slung the kid over to her. It wasn't until she was down in the kitchen and noticed that the crying had stopped that she thought that giving the baby to a stranger had been an incredibly stupid thing to do and her mother would kill her if she ever found out.

She ran back upstairs and found the lady sitting in the rocking chair, cooing at the baby who smiled at her adoringly.

"Who's a beautiful boy, who's a beautiful boy?" the lady was asking. Alex smiled, knowing it was him.

Lucy handed her the bottle.

"It's cold," said the lady.

"That's okay, he'll eat anything."

He took it and started sucking hungrily.

"Look," said the lady, amazed, "he's trying to hold it! What a good boy."

"You're good with kids," Lucy said. "You have any?"

The lady shot her an exasperated look and rolled her eyes. "No. But I got a little brother. He's ten years old now and a real monster, but when he was a baby he was almost as cute as you!" She was talking to the baby again and the baby was laughing. "No, he says, nobody is as cute as me, I'm the cutest."

Alex loved this.

She asked what his name was and Lucy told her. The lady said her name was Jesse and she wanted to know if Lucy was in college. She said she was, in her Sophomore year.

"Oh great, what's it like, do you like it? I've been thinking of going, but I can't decide, I just can't decide."

"It's fun, I like it. I think it's cool that you're thinking of going."

Jesse looked a little surprised. "Thanks."

"Mind if I ask you why you didn't go before?"

She shrugged. "Well you know, I have to finish high school."

Lucy nodded. She admired the lady for trying to start over. She'd obviously had some tough times.

The lady stood up and walked to the window, looking at the Stuarts' house next door.

"That's the Harrigan's house." She turned to Lucy. "That <u>is</u> the Harrigan's house, isn't it?"

"No, the Stuarts live there."

"But it looks the same, everything looks the same." She sat in the rocking chair again, still cradling the baby in her arms. "God, there must really be something wrong with me." She looked at the bruise on her hand. "I don't remember how any of this happened. And my house is supposed to be here." She looked out the back window. "There's the eucalyptus tree. But Christ, it's so much taller. My house is supposed to be right here. How long has this house been here?"

Lucy shrugged. "I don't know. Long time. Since we moved here."

"When was that?"

"Eighty."

"Eighty what?"

"Nineteen-eighty."

The lady stood up and handed Alex to her. "I think you better take the baby."

Then she went out the door and started down the stairs. Lucy followed her, calling out, "You're sure you're okay, you're sure you don't want me to call somebody?"

"I don't think there's anybody to call, Lucy."

Lucy was running down the stairs then, the baby bouncing on her shoulder. "Wait a minute, I just remembered. You've been here before, right?"

She was at the front door now, and when she turned there was a shining of tears on her eyes. "I don't know," she said, steadily.

"You have, yeah. Dad didn't really tell me what it was about, but he gave me a number to call." She was in the kitchen now, rummaging through the dozens of notes stuck to the refrigerator by little magnets shaped like letters of the alphabet. "Here it is," she plucked one from under the Z. "Carl Robson."

"Carl?" she said, and her voice wasn't so dead this time. "I'd like to call Carl."

Lucy ran into the living room, happy to have found something to help her. "Come on, the phone's in here. Don't worry, everything's going to be alright."

But she didn't follow. Lucy went back and found her in the front hall in front of a big mirror, looking at her face with an expression of revulsion, which puzzled Lucy because, except for the black eye and the scratch, she didn't look that bad.

"I don't think so," the lady said, tracing the lines of her face with her fingertips, "I really don't think so."

TWENTY-FOUR

On his way from his house to the Fletcher's he had to drive past an old park where he used to play when he was a kid. He remembered when they put in all the equipment – brand-new stuff all shaped like rockets and jet planes. It was rusted now – the paint was peeling off the jet plane swings; they'd had to wrap fencing around the top part of the big rocket ship jungle gym. Had somebody fallen from it, he wondered, or was the wire there just to give it reinforcement? As he recalled, kids used to jump from side to side up there to make the whole thing sway dangerously. What was the point of play if it wasn't dangerous?

Frank wasn't saying anything; he was just looking out the window, tapping his finger on the leather seat, trying to get there faster, trying to hurry up the rhythm of time.

After Jesse had called they'd been paralyzed with fear and helplessness. There could have been any number of innocent reasons for the disconnection; they could only come up with guilty ones.

So they sat for what seemed like hours, but was only about thirty-five minutes before another call came. This time they both grabbed different phones and listened together.

They were at the house now. Carl was glad this daughter had shown up and happened to be there when Jesse came, because she seemed less paranoid and a lot more sympathetic than her parents. She met them at the door with a six month old baby in her arms, both of them smiling and enjoying the diversion. She said that Jesse was in the family room watching TV and offered them Cokes.

Carl glanced at the big mirror in the hall and he gasped – an audible gasp, a sound he could never remember making before. He could see Jesse in the mirror – she was watching TV in an easy chair, her legs curled up next to her and munching from a bag of Fritos.

He felt the shock of her coming back to him all over again. The sense of past rushing up and embracing him. He'd forgotten all of that in the desire to find her, to make sure she was safe. He'd forgotten the violence of the sight of her.

If it was a shock for him he could only imagine what it must have done to Frank, who was seeing her come back from the dead. But he didn't talk about the pain or the shock or the relief. All he said was, "She's hurt."

"Yeah," said the girl, "she came here like that. She doesn't remember how it happened. She seems confused about a lot of things to tell you the truth."

"I know," Frank said.

Carl went in to her and she looked up at him and smiled. "Hi, Carl," she said. She looked at him oddly, "Who the hell are all these people on Star Trek?"

He was kneeling next to her, looking at the welt on her face and swollen purple eye. "Are you okay?"

"Great. You sure you're okay, you don't look so good."

"I'm hung over. Jesse, I want you to come meet a friend of mine named Frank."

"Hi, Frank," she said. Frank didn't say anything.

Jesse kissed the baby goodbye and they thanked the girl. On the way to the car Jesse pulled Carl ahead a little and asked if his friend was okay. Carl said, "Sure, why do you ask?"

"It looks like he's crying," she said, making an embarrassed face.

TWENTY-FIVE

She had collected another car. It was a white Volvo parked in front of the house with a metal frame around the license plate that said 'Damn I'm Good.' Frank found the keys in her pocket and drove it back to Carl's house. What with the rental, the BMW, the Mercedes, and the Volvo, it looked like there was a party going on at Carl's house.

The three men sat around the kitchen in a state of confusion usually only achieved at parties that last into the early hours of the morning. Carl was the host, so he busied himself making dinner, failing at any attempts to make conversation, only able to list in his mind the myriad of things they couldn't talk about.

Where had Jesse been? No good asking, she was the last person who'd know. Who or what had hurt her? Bringing up her injuries only upset her – how could a person get hurt that way and not even remember how it happened? What was Frank thinking and feeling to see her brought back to life? But they couldn't talk about Jesse's forgotten past with her there in the room. Besides did Carl really want to know what Frank was feeling? Not with Jesse hanging on to Carl, nuzzling his neck, giggling in his ear. He tried to make her stop, for Frank's sake, but it's hard to come up with a good reason to stop your girlfriend from kissing you. Glancing back occasionally at Frank and looking embarrassed only seemed to goad her on, as if she thought it was cute and a little naughty to get Carl excited in front of this friend of his she'd never met. And how to explain to Frank that she just thought they were still boyfriend and girlfriend, that it was all perfectly innocent? Or imperfectly so, anyway.

For his part, Frank seemed a master of the situation. After the initial tears, the shock of seeing her back from her watery death, he fell into a behavior guaranteed to put her at ease. Introducing himself as Carl's friend, making no pretense to previous acquaintance with her, she found nothing threatening about him. And, after the brief separation while they drove their respective cars to Carl's place, he introduced himself again, not needing to be prompted; seeming to know in his blood how long her memory would last. What's more, there was nothing forced in his re-introduction, no sense that it hurt him or that it was an effort. An ignorant witness, observing the scene, would take it at face value, just as Jesse did.

In conversation he had an instinctive mastery of what subjects were contained in the bubble of her world. He asked about the food they were eating, the look of the room, the birds outside. Engaging in the friendly banter strangers have about the here and now, avoiding all topics that might bring up the larger questions of time and experience.

And Jesse liked him. Laughed at his jokes, smiled at Carl once or twice as if to say, 'this guy's cool, where've you been keeping him so long?' It was the sort of first meeting that could grow into a real friendship.

Except it wouldn't.

After falling asleep on the sofa watching <u>Dr. Zhivago</u> on the, to her, futuristic marvel of the VCR, she drifted awake again and smiled curiously at Frank. Again he introduced himself, apologizing for waking her. She drifted off again, snuggling against Carl, who eased away from her as her breathing settled into the steady rhythm of sleep.

"She still thinks we're…" Carl started to explain.

"I know, it's wonderful." Frank seemed sincere. "I haven't seen her this at ease in months. It's terrific to see her with someone she knows. She finally feels safe."

So there was to be no mention of the physical contact. No expression of any jealousy he might be feeling. Carl had no problem with that. Hypocrisy makes the world comfortable.

They tucked her into bed in the guest room downstairs and she woke up in a drowsy way, wondering why she wasn't going home. Carl reminded her that her parents thought she was spending the night at Annie's house.

At that, she pulled him down to her and kissed him, her breath hot in his ear. He pulled away and said he'd sneak in later, when the house was quiet. Then he stumbled out of the room, past Frank who stood in the doorway, unnervingly at ease.

"Look," Carl said when they were back in the living room, "I don't want you to think there's anything going on."

"No," Frank dismissed it.

"I would never take advantage…"

"Of course not."

"But you have to humor her."

"I understand."

Carl switched off the set as Omar Sharif was dying on the bus.

Frank dropped a piece of paper on the coffee table. It was a car registration with an address and name: Theodore Ryan.

"What's that?'

"The guy who owns the Volvo. I think we should go see him."

"What for?"

"Haven't you asked yourself where she was between when she fell off the boat and you found her in your backyard?"

"Of course."

"Maybe this guy knows."

"Why would he know?"

"Maybe he doesn't. Let's find out."

"It's a waste of time."

Frank stood up, bursting forth with a sudden anger which seemed to come out of nowhere, but which must have been building for a long time. He was clearly a person who seldom felt such anger, so his body hardly knew what to do with it. It jerked his body in sudden, awkward spasms. "Carl, somebody beat her up. Somebody hurt her."

"She'll be all right."

"All right? Who knows what he did to her?"

Well, she doesn't, Carl thought to himself. And, if you discount the minor physical injury, was it really possible to hurt her? Can you inflict psychological and emotional trauma on someone if they forget it completely and immediately? Had the disease rendered her superhuman, impervious to the slings and arrows that pierced lesser mortals? Could she brush off an assault the way Superman brushed off hooligans' bullets?

"She's got on different clothes." And this seemed the greatest outrage of all.

"We don't know," Carl said. "Maybe this guy helped her. Found her and took her for coffee and she ran off with his car."

"Then let's return it. I'm going. You want to come?"

The storm of anger blew off as quickly as it had come, replaced by a boyish grin on Frank's face that seemed to say, 'c'mon, it'll be fun.'

Well, going to see this Ryan would be flat out stupid. Nothing more than a delaying action to put off the inevitable point when they'd have to give up this game and sit down and figure out what was best for Jesse and themselves.

"Sure," he said.

TWENTY-SIX

When Jesse woke up, she found a note on the bed.

"*Had to go out, but will be back real soon. Just make your-self comfortable – my parents are gone for the weekend. If you're confused about anything don't worry, I'll explain it all when I come back. In the meantime just make yourself at home, watch TV or something, but please don't leave the house, I don't have an extra key.*

I love you."

It was signed "*Carl*" and it had the little x's with exclamation points after them which stood for more than kisses.

She found two copies of the letter in every room in the house.

TWENTY-SEVEN

Ryan sat with one leg hooked over the arm of his sofa enjoying the indescribable luxury of having a conversation upon which his freedom was not at stake. A conversation that was a bit of greasing of the wheels of human contact. A conversation none of the participants gave a damn about.

"I'm formulating a hard and fast rule. I'm calling it Ryan's rule of Baseball – the more money you pay them, the worse they play."

"Look at Strawberry," Carl said.

"My point, exactly. Love of money is the root of all bad Baseball," Ryan said. Ryan had no knowledge of or interest in sports and consequently he enjoyed discussing it immensely. It gave him a chance to enjoy the structure of inter-personal communication without being distracted by meaning.

There was a glory in sitting here engaged in aimless chatter on the evening of the very day in which his freedom had almost been taken from him. More than once he'd had to choke off a victorious yelp that he found swelling in his chest.

It had been a tense moment when they'd first appeared at the door, of course. He'd been sitting in his easy chair listening to Bruce Springsteen on the stereo. This was something he never did at five o'clock, even on his days off. There was always Gloria bustling about the house, making him do things or feel guilty about not doing things. Even if he had been able to put a CD on and sit in his chair, it would have been pointless to try to listen to it. She would have resented him his peace – she hated people doing nothing. The best he could do was pretend to read the paper, or, better yet, some book connected with work. But with the words in front of his eyes he couldn't concentrate on the music, and with the music going he couldn't concentrate on the words. So he would hang suspended between listening and reading, doing neither, but racing awkwardly from one to the other in a vain attempt to look occupied.

With the house to himself, he could actually do one thing at a time. So he was somewhat irritated when they appeared at his door, his stolen car parked on the street behind them, eyeing him like hillbilly brothers accusing him of doing God-knows-what to their sister. He recognized Carl and vice versa and for a moment their recognition seemed to prove something and Ryan had an impulse to confess everything.

Instead, he thanked them for returning his car and asked them where they'd found it. He said he had been foolish enough to leave the keys in it at the school lot and when he'd tried to go home it was gone.

He was gratified to see them deflate. They might have turned to go then, but the one armed fellow (in his initial nervousness Ryan had quite missed his name) looked so disappointed he seemed almost faint. Ryan invited them in for a sit down and a drink. Carl seemed hesitant, but One Arm's condition left little room for argument.

They settled One Arm down in an easy chair and he said he needed nothing but a chance to breathe and proceeded to do so with much noise and concentration. Ryan asked if they'd found the woman they were looking for. Carl explained that she had shown up with his car and that she'd been beaten badly. Ryan was shocked. He couldn't believe something like that would happen near the school, but he supposed anything was possible these days.

Carl didn't seem to want to say much more about that, so Ryan and Carl shared a beer while the color returned to One

Arm's cheeks and they discussed baseball. Carl shot occasional glances at One Arm, as if impatient for him to get back on his feet, but Ryan was in no hurry for them to go. He remembered part of an old quote about how entertaining friends in one's house gave every man a taste of what it's like to be a king. Well, these weren't even his friends but that was just how he felt – like a king who was free to do as he pleased, even if it was only to waste a few precious moments of life discussing the idiocy of Fred Clair.

Just a few hours ago time had been a more precious commodity. He'd been sitting in Presser's office sweating, afraid that it wouldn't occur to anyone to actually check the tunnel. Presser seemed intent on simply lecturing him again on how difficult all this was for Presser and how he believed in Ryan but could not actually do anything to help him.

Finally Ryan had to suggest looking, which was more obvious and less elegant than he would have liked, but Presser didn't seem suspicious. And when he found the joints and the rest, Presser seemed considerably relieved. The whole affair could now be safely ignored.

The part Ryan liked best was his own indignant objection to the searching of Jenny's locker. Vice-Principal Estelman was the one who suggested it, and although Ryan usually found him repulsive, he could have kissed him then.

By that point Jenny's parents had been brought in too. They were briefly cowed by the joints found in the wall, but they bounced back, saying it didn't prove anything, it was only a coincidence. But they were already defending themselves.

So when Estelman brought up the idea of searching the locker and Ryan opposed it on Constitutional and moral grounds, Kallen was placed in the position of either agreeing with his enemy or demanding that his daughter's locker be searched. He did the latter, saying he had faith in her and knew they wouldn't find anything.

Ryan kept up his speech about how children were entitled to the same rights of privacy as the rest of society all the way through the opening of the locker. Then he looked just as shocked as everybody else.

Ryan remembered Jenny crying in his office one day about her father. He'd never hit her, of course, but he did always seem to disapprove of her. No matter how well she did in school, he only spotted the failures – he'd harp more on one B than on a slew of A's. Her whole struggle to succeed and do well in school was another of those pathetic attempts to gain approval from someone who preferred to expect the worst.

Ryan knew there were a million deep psychological causes for this relationship, but he didn't care to find out what they were. All that mattered now was that once the situation had stopped being the simple one of his daughter being raped by the perverted teacher, once it had all become a bit more complex, it was easier for him to blame her than to try to sort it all out.

Her mother stood up for her at first, but it began to sound more like someone making excuses. And her defense of her daughter's character was further hampered by being seconded at every turn by Ryan. Kallen simply grew quiet now, and muttered to himself with an embarrassed air.

An aunt or a grandparent finally brought Jenny into the office. At first this frightened Ryan a little, but once their eyes met it was all going to be over soon. He could see she was sorry she started this and was ready to take any route out he could give her.

So they asked her about the drugs and at that she looked at him and her look was very different. It was angry and hurt and he felt a little guilty, till he remembered that she'd almost got him sent to prison. She denied knowing anything about the drugs.

He spoke to her very gently, without moving toward her. He reminded her of their friendship and told her not to be afraid, that they all just wanted to help her. He also told her that he didn't blame her for any of this. He just thought she'd feel better if she told the truth.

When she looked at him that time he realized that she hated him now and that surprised him. Then he decided that it was only a natural reaction to preserve her dignity, so he didn't blame her for that either.

She spoke quickly and bitterly and before he heard her words he'd started to feel frightened that her intensity might turn the others against him again.

"Okay, I'll tell you the truth, if that's what you want. I've been on drugs for months and when Mr. Ryan found out and tried to stop me I decided to get him in trouble."

There was no forgiveness in her eyes, so Ryan kept waiting for a trap to be sprung. It couldn't be that simple.

But the others pounced with relief. She was scolded for the damage she'd almost done to a fine teacher, condemned for her behavior. Estelman was for calling the police. Presser demanded she seek psychiatric care. Her mother wept and her father looked like he planned to fulfill Ryan's prophecy of child beating as soon as he got her home.

And all the while she kept looking at Ryan, smiling in triumph as if the trap had already caught him.

Talk of police faded. It was agreed that she get psychiatric help. There was a doctor Presser knew who specialized in treating teen behavior disorders. It would mean missing a few classes, of course, but under the circumstances it might be better for her to take some time away from school altogether. There was obviously more to this than just drugs. The girl was nearly friendless, they decided, and her attempt to destroy the one teacher who tried to reach out and help her showed deep anti-social tendencies.

Kallen avoided Ryan's eyes on the way out, but Mrs. Kallen made a clumsy effort at an apology. Ryan wished her well.

He kept thinking about Jenny's smile all through Presser's apology – or rather his insistence that he'd never doubted Ryan for an instant, which Ryan knew to be true. What was left unsaid was the fact that he would never have stuck his neck out to defend him if the facts hadn't been so overwhelming.

So he was back home and safe, with the added advantage of his wife being gone. She'd be back when she heard no more of this. She might even believe him now. She might not. It was difficult living with someone who knew you that well.

But he kept thinking about that smile and why Jenny kept looking like she thought she'd won, when everyone was so obviously believing his story. Then it came to him. She was deliberately sacrificing herself for him, throwing herself on the spear of his story, with the idea that he was going to suffer from guilt at his mistreatment of her. No doubt she was picturing him now, twisting in torment at the price he'd paid for his freedom.

He was glad that this fantasy was giving her some happiness in a difficult time, but mostly he just wondered how he could have fallen for a girl that naïve.

Drifting back from these thoughts, he found himself discussing President Clinton's Hollywood ties and how they were damaging him. Carl seemed particularly vehement about this. He noticed that One Arm was gone from the room and vaguely remembered him excusing himself to use the john.

"What he doesn't understand," Carl was saying, "is how much America hates us. They watch our shows, they go to our movies, but they just don't trust us. They think we're irresponsible, left wing, perverts. And they're right."

From all the 'us's' and 'ours', Ryan supposed that Carl must work in show business and that he didn't care for it much. He wondered if he could dust off that old spec script he'd written a few years back and show it to him.

"I don't suppose you people ever read outside scripts..."

Carl reacted with a sharp intake of breath that made Ryan think he'd asked the wrong question, until he realized that he was staring at something across the room. Ryan turned and saw One Arm holding something made of dirty white cloth in his hand.

Then he remembered the dress. Frank was holding Jesse's white dress.

"Where'd you find that?" Carl was asking.

"The trash."

They were both in front of him now and he tried to fight hard to keep his leg still hanging casually over the arm of his sofa.

"She was here," Carl said.

He couldn't think of a way to deny it. "No," he said.

Ryan involuntarily pulled his leg down, thought about putting it back but decided it wouldn't look casual now.

"What did you do to her?" One Arm asked.

"I don't know what you're talking about, that's my wife's dress."

"She was here."

"You guys want to get out of here or am I going to call the police?"

Carl laughed, "You?"

"Well, somebody stole my car."

"Did you hurt her?"

One Arm moved in on him and Ryan clambered off the sofa in an almost casual way. He didn't like this guy. His whole approach to getting out of trouble was based on the idea that what people really wanted was for things to calm down and be normal and this guy didn't seem to care about that.

"I don't have to listen to this," he said, knowing it was very weak.

The one hand reached out and touched Ryan's throat, just the fingertips touching, and somehow the gentleness of the move made it more shocking. "Look at me. Did you hurt her?" He did look and the eyes he saw were dead inside and Ryan knew he was dealing with a crazy.

He backed away from the fingertips and into a wall, knocking a picture frame crooked with the back of his head.

"All right, she was here. Thought she could clean up, put on a change of clothes, then I'd call you guys. Well, she goes crazy. You know she's crazy. She attacked me." Here he showed them the cut on his forehead, wishing it was larger. "So I had to calm her down, defend myself. She broke away, stole my car and that's it."

One Arm kept looking at him and Ryan knew he hadn't believed a word of it, which struck him as rather funny since it was the closest thing to the truth he'd said all day.

"I don't think so," One Arm said. "I think you've had her here since yesterday. Why did you hurt her? Or do you just do it for the fun of it?"

"What are you talking about?" Ryan turned to Carl, as a sensible ally. "What is he talking about? Is everybody you know crazy?"

Carl didn't answer, but One Arm didn't shut up. "You found out what was wrong with her, so you thought it would be okay, isn't that right? You could play any little game you wanted and it would just wash away. But she wouldn't put up with it, would she? What did she do to make you kick her in the face?"

Ryan pushed past him to the center of the room. "Shut up you son of a bitch, this is bullshit. My wife was here last night, you can't prove any of this, it's bullshit. The only thing you can prove is that your crazy bitch stole my car; you want me to call the police on that? Do you?"

His hand was on the phone and to his amazement he felt them back down, saw them step back. He pushed it further.

"I'm calling. I'm calling right now."

He felt like he was holding a cross out to a vampire. One Arm left – just turned and walked out of the house. Carl gave him a wonderfully impotent snort and left too.

His hand was shaking when he took it off the phone and the room seemed to vibrate with their absence. He wadded up the dress, tossed it in the fireplace, got a can of lighter fluid from under the sink, doused it, then set it on fire.

He squatted in front of the screen and watched, arms around his knees, his face hot from the flames. Springsteen was still on the stereo but it was one of those damned factory-closing-down songs and he didn't enjoy it.

TWENTY-EIGHT

Carl leaned on the door jam and watched her sleep. He had no idea what time of night it was and he was afraid to look at his watch and find out. Every hour or so, one of them would get up from the kitchen table and go in to look at her, never telling the other what he was doing. Then, comforted by the sight of her sleeping, he would go downstairs and start to talk again.

Bottles of Corona lined the table, though neither of them were drinkers. A few of the bottles swirled with the smoke of dying cigarette butts, though they'd both stopped smoking years ago. They'd gone from beer to wine to coffee, but still the talk wouldn't end.

Sitting in stunned silence on the way home from Ryan's, they had begun to talk, overlapping each other in waves of enthusiasm, as soon as they'd walked into Carl's house. Fishing the keys to the many cars out of their pockets (they couldn't dare leave any in the house for Jesse to pilfer) and tossing them on the counter, they immediately began to rehash the interview.

"Could you believe it?"

"I couldn't believe it."

"The way he stood there and…"

"The gall of the son of a…"

"Did he think we'd believe that…"

"Does he think we're idiots?"

"Still, I almost believed him."

"He thinks we're idiots."

"When did you stop believing him?"

"When he opened the door."

"Is that why you pretended to get sick?"

"I had to get a way in."

"That was fast. You thought fast."

"I had to get a way in."

"And when you brought the dress out. You should've seen his face."

"I saw his face."

A drag on a stale cigarette found in the back of a cupboard. Carl looking at Frank through the smoke.

"Do you think he really did anything to her?"

And silence and a beer and going round it all again, again and again, they felt sick from the circular motion.

"He could have done anything to her."

"No way of knowing."

"She doesn't even know."

Now it was Frank's turn to suck on the year old Marlboro and feel his eyes burn from the smoke. "I know what you're thinking. What does it matter what he did to her? She's an Etch-A-Sketch – draw whatever you want on her, shake her and it's gone…Well, it matters to me."

But what could they do? Go to the police? With what? And what about Martin? The police would give her back to him. Would she be safe there? Round and round.

And taking turns going in to look at her. And wanting to fall onto a pillow and sleep. But no, the answer is close. Just have to keep talking.

Finally, out of nausea, out of a feeling that if he went over this ground one more time he might literally vomit, Carl asked Frank a question he'd been afraid to ask. How did they become lovers?

Frank looked up from urging Mr. Coffee onward.

"You're surprised she'd be unfaithful? I was. She believed in marriage and she hated cheating."

"But love is always infidelity, isn't it? Always a betrayal of someone or something. Even with your first girl, when you're seventeen and living at home, you're still cheating. Cheating on your parents. Pretending to be a child with them and a man with her. Having to hide the smile on your face and the scent of her on your body. And all that hiding making it so much more precious, so much more exciting."

"And you're cheating on your friends too. Pretending you're still one of the gang, when all you are is her lover and you could care less about any of them."

"And it doesn't matter how old you are, or how free you are, you still cheat. A single man with a job in love with a single girl, he's still unfaithful. He's cheating every time he drives to work and pretends to go through the old routine, while, in his mind he's really with her, rushing to her, flowing all over her."

"Just walking down the street, pretending to be a regular human being, he's betraying all the other human beings around him. Because he's nothing like them. He's not walking next to them at all. He's not even there. He's with her."

The old cat jumped onto the counter and Frank began to pet her. "And we were in our thirties. Well into the Age of Boredom, when nothing is new."

"Now I'm not being self-pitying, it's simply true. New-ness, or whatever you want to call it, becomes a very scarce commodity after thirty. I think that's unfair. If I were in charge of the human life span, I'd make sure to budget new-ness much more selectively, to ration it out. As it is now, it's almost used up in the first three years of life. By then you've seen for the first time, tasted for the first time, held something for the first time. Learned to walk, talk, go to the bathroom. What have you got to look forward to that can compare with that? Sure, there's school. Making friends. Falling in love. Learning to drive. Sex. Learning a trade. That has to carry you for the next twenty-five years. But after that? What's the new excitement? Mastering your home computer? Figuring out how to work CompuServe?"

"Now, if it were up to me, I'd parcel it out. So that, say, at thirty-five we just learned how to go on the potty. Imagine the feeling of accomplishment! They'd have office parties. 'Did you hear? The Vice-President in Charge of Overseas Development just went a whole week without his diaper. We're buying him a gift.' It'd be beautiful." Frank laughed and the cat jumped to the floor with a loud thump and a liquid grunt.

"So that's why you did it," Carl said, "because you were bored?"

"Well, yeah, but I can tell from your tone that I'm not explaining this well. Look at it from her point of view. She's not happy in her marriage. Not unhappy exactly, but not happy. He doesn't want kids, so that's nothing to look forward to. Her life is chock full of quiet tedium. Suddenly, she falls in love. And sure, there's the excitement of being with her lover, but there's also the excitement of not being with him. Of waiting and going on with her ordinary life. And all that dullness now becomes part of the drama. Because that's her cover story. All the dreary anguish and monotony that fills ninety-eight percent of her life is electrified with meaning, since it now serves as the perfect camouflage to hide the two percent of passion."

"And, yes, she felt guilt and, yes, she felt shame. But those are powerful emotions too, and were all part of the glorious transformation of a featureless, bland life into an adventure."

"For you too?" Carl asked.

"Of course," Frank said, off hand. "For me it started much earlier. I'd been in love with her for about two years. Apologizing love. Really gut-wrenching stuff. My brother's wife. Around her all the time. Longing to touch her. Feeling pain, real pain, in my stomach when I was around her. But not wanting to be anywhere else. And loving every minute of it, don't get me wrong. All that pain made life worth living."

"It's like when I lost my arm. I was fifteen. Martin had just gotten his driver's license and he took me out joy riding with some friends. Drinking a lot of beer, of course. Plowed into a telephone pole. I had my arm crooked out the window on the passenger's side, like a real grown-up. And then, well, I didn't have my arm anymore."

"And before I knew what had happened, Martin was crying over me. Really crying, only time I ever saw him do that. And for years after that, I was the center of everything. I was the injured boy in the hospital. The handicapped child. The patient in physical therapy. The child overcoming his disability. Every accomplishment was over-praised, every failure was explained away. Well, it ruined my character, let me tell you and I wouldn't have had it any other way. Who wouldn't give their right arm to be treated like something special?"

"Well, being in love with Jesse, that felt the same way. It made me special. I was the man in love. The heartbroken man. The rejected suitor. It was wonderful."

"And then, and yes, I'm finally answering your question, we went to my cabin in the desert one weekend. She knew how I felt about her and I think it flattered her, although she pretended to feel sorry for me. Anyway, we were all supposed to go to the cabin, Martin and Jesse and me. But at the last minute, Martin couldn't go – he had to fly to New York on business. So Jesse decided to go on her own. I thought that meant something. It's a three-hour drive to the cabin, with her sitting right next to me, and all the while I kept thinking maybe it meant something. We got there. I took those pictures of her in the desert."

"Then it happened."

"We made love all weekend. We never stopped. I don't think two people have ever done anything like it in recorded history. I remember every second. I could close my eyes now and relive it all. And that's good, because she's forgotten. So if I forget any of it, then it's just gone forever."

"When the weekend was over, driving home, she swore that was it. That it would never happen again. I was terrified she meant it. But she came to my house a few days later. And after <u>that</u> she said it would never happen again and I was terrified again and I spent the next eleven months bouncing between terror and ecstasy and you can't tell me that a happy marriage and beautiful children have anything on that."

"Then she began to forget things and you know all about that. Eventually there came a day when she forgot we were lovers. I can still feel that particular candle being snuffed out. I almost killed myself. Sometimes I wish I had. I'm sure you do too, now that I've talked this much. Except," and he looked down the hall toward her room, "she still needs me."

Carl, now wishing to get off this subject, tried to leap back to the old one. "But what do we do?"

Frank stood up. "I'm going to talk to Martin. Take a look at that letter. See if Jeff really wrote it."

"Now?"

Frank smiled. "Why not? Do him good to get up early. What else do you want me to ask him?"

"Find out why he lied about Jeff being here. Find out if he knows where he is. And if he's okay."

Frank looked at him and spoke with unexpected emotion. "If anything happened to Jeff it would kill her. Absolutely kill her."

"Yeah, well...if we're even a little right about Martin...you be careful."

"Of my brother?" he laughed. "Don't worry, he won't hurt me."

"Carl?" A voice spoke from the hall.

He turned in surprise to see Jesse behind him, blinking her eyes in the corridor. "What time is it?"

"I'm about to take you home. This is my uncle Frank Ackerman."

"Hi, Uncle Frank."

"Hello."

"Can I get a Coke?"

"Sure, Jesse. Frank's just leaving."

"Bye, Frank."

She grabbed her Coke and padded off down the hall. Frank followed her with his eyes till he couldn't see her anymore. Then he looked at Carl.

"You're sleeping with her, aren't you?"

It was past four in the morning, Carl had five beers in him and he wasn't sure he could have lied to this man anyway. He didn't say anything, but that said it all.

"That's alright," Frank said, quietly, "It must make her feel at home. I could never do that."

He turned and walked out the door. Carl went to the window and watched him climb into one of the cars – he'd chosen the Mercedes from the school lot, Carl noted. As he climbed into the car, his face looked ghostly in the momentary flash of the interior light. Then he disappeared in darkness.

Carl went into the guest bedroom and held her. They made love and he kept nothing inside himself. He didn't picture her at eighteen; he loved her as she was and she loved him as she could. When it was over he lay next to her, his head on her breasts, his mind wonderfully empty.

"Carl," she said. "I have to tell you. Don't be mad, but I think I'm pregnant."

He held her so hard that she laughed for a second, till she heard the sniffling and knew he was crying. She patted his head and shushed him and told him it would be all right.

In his mind, he swore he would never let go of her.

TWENTY-NINE

They did everything in cars.

Talked in cars. Partied in cars. Listened to music in cars. Fought in cars. Made love in cars.

And, remember, this was in the days before the bucket seat was standard. Back then, the front seat of a car was a roomy sofa; a teenager's living room. No seatbelts automatically wrapped around you as you started the car. You were free to move as you wished.

And they wished. Sitting sideways, facing each other, discussing politics and the world and how the Republicans could never come back now that Nixon had fallen. Reclining in each other's arms, flesh touching where clothing had been opened, watching the stars over the mountains through the windshield. She sitting in the middle of the bench seat, pressing herself next to him as he drove, arm around his neck, hand in his lap or on his chest, breathing into his ear, never letting him go.

Are bucket seats worth the price we've paid?

"Rihannon" was on the car stereo. Carl sat with his back against the door, his knees drawn up on the seat between them. Jesse was smoking a cigarette and had the door half open to let out the smoke. The car didn't beep to tell them the door was open. Cars didn't talk back to you in those days.

"I have some money…" He said. "enough to…I can help."

Carl didn't know the right words to use. He wanted desperately to do the right thing and these days he was pretty sure 'the right thing' meant offering to pay for the abortion.

"How?" she asked, exhaling smoke dramatically. She kept acting like she was alone in this. Didn't she realize it was his problem too?

"I can take you to a clinic," he said. "I'll pay," he added quickly, hating the way it sounded. As if he were offering to pick up the check for a pizza.

She looked over at him from across the long length of the front seat. "So you want to kill it?" she asked.

This took him totally by surprise. It was one of the phrases that stayed with him for the rest of his life. One that floated up to his consciousness, jerking him awake as he drifted off to sleep in many beds over many years. One he kept composing new answers for, much better than the one he gave.

"Kill what?" he said, with a nervous laugh.

"The baby."

This put things in a wholly new perspective. He'd viewed the pregnancy as an unforeseen problem, an illness to be overcome, a tragedy to be survived.

That idiotic nervous laugh again. "What else can we do?"

"Is that what you want?"

He couldn't reply. There was a gulf between them now, and he couldn't be sure that anything he might say wouldn't make it wider.

"What do you want?" he asked her.

She didn't answer.

"I mean, do you want to have it?" He knew she was Catholic, but never thought she was <u>Catholic</u>.

"I already have it. I've already got it, Carl. The question is, what do we do…with it."

"Well…um…" There were four goals in his mind. To get her to stop talking foolishly. To get her to agree to an abortion. Not to lose her. To find the magic words that would make things what they were before.

"Do you think we're a little young to think about getting married?" he asked.

"Weren't we thinking about it?"

"Well, sure, but in the long run. And I'll marry you right now, if you want. I will. But we were talking about after college and all. Weren't we? And you're the one who wasn't even sure we should go to the same college." He played that last part like it was a trump card. "You said we should see other people, so we know it's right."

"And you still want to do that?"

"I never wanted to do that. You were the one. Stop acting like this is all my fault. I am not deserting you."

"If I decided to have the baby, what would you do?"

"Oh, man, do you think this is fair?"

"No."

"Do you really think it's fair…"

"No."

"…to ask me to throw my life away, just 'cause…"

"Somebody's life's gonna get thrown away, Carl. We just have to decide whose."

"Oh, now that's stupid, and you know it." He couldn't believe this was Jesse talking. She was the radical, firebrand feminist of the school. He remembered her rage when Lyn Bushnell started going through the cafeteria, passing out pamphlets with pictures of aborted fetuses. The screaming match they'd had by the lunch line; Lyn declaiming about promiscuity and the sanctity of life, Jesse passionately standing up for a woman's right to control her own body. He'd never loved her more.

And now she was talking about life and killing.

"I'm not saying it's fair," she was looking straight at him for the first time that night, "and I'm not saying it's right. All I'm saying is, if I decide to have the baby, if I don't tell a soul who the father is, if I never ask a thing from you, if I promise never to even call you again, would you still say you'd marry me?"

He looked right back at her. "Of course."

But she knew he was lying.

She put out her cigarette, opened the car door and walked away. He didn't call her and, like she promised, she never called him.

THIRTY

In many cultures there exists a belief that one must leave the world as one entered it. The eunuchs of Imperial China, advisors to the Emperor kept their testicles in earthen jars to be buried with them. For if they attempted to enter the Kingdom of Heaven without all their original parts, the way would be barred to them.

Frank Ackerman's arm, what was left of it after the accident, was disposed of as medical waste. He could never enter the Kingdom of Heaven.

THIRTY-ONE

In the morning they got up and fed the birds. The feeders were empty, so the birds were waiting impatiently on the power lines. After refilling them, Carl and Jesse stood back in the patio and watched the turtledoves and sparrows feast. A scrub jay chased a mockingbird through the upper branches. The canary didn't show up and that disappointed Carl, because he wanted to surprise Jesse with it. That was one thing about their relationship; he could never run out of ways to surprise her.

He made breakfast and thought about their future together. He hadn't really seen how possible it all was until he'd understood Frank's plight. That was impossibility; Carl only had to deal with inconveniences.

One plan was to quit his job, which felt like a small sacrifice, sell the house and move to a cheaper state or country where he could retire on his savings and spend all his time with her.

Of course, the time could come when she'd require more expensive care and then his savings might not be enough. So the other plan was to keep his job, or at least free-lance to keep money coming in. What he'd do with her when he was at work wasn't so clear. Perhaps lock her up in the attic like Rochester's wife.

He brought a plate of eggs and sausage into the living room where she was flipping through the channels with the remote.

"Jesus. There must be fifty stations here."

"Forty-two."

"What kind of TV is this?" She stopped on MTV. "Who is that?"

"Eric Clapton."

"Gawd, he looks like an accountant."

She switched to the weather and wolfed down her eggs. They really impressed her. She'd never dreamed that Carl would think of cooking breakfast for her, much less do it well. The news came on, but she didn't listen. Why get depressed by a bunch of disasters and fires and suicides when your boyfriend, who usually forgets to even send you a card on Valentine's Day, just made you the best cheese omelet you ever had?

She smiled at Carl, but he was staring at the news very intently. She looked to the TV to see what had captured his attention. Something about a fire in Pasadena. Some guy had been found burned up in his house. They thought it was suicide or arson. The body was pretty charred, but they could identify it because it only had one arm. Jesse didn't think that made too much sense.

She switched the channel to a re-run of I Love Lucy.

Carl was still staring at the TV and she thought he was looking a little funny. Then he got up and just walked outside without saying anything. She finished her eggs and remembered that this was the one where they were in Hollywood and Lucy stole John Wayne's footprint from Grauman's Chinese. She checked Carl again through the French doors and saw him sitting with his face in his hands out on one of the lawn chairs.

She put her plate down and walked out to him, not knowing what to say exactly. She'd never seen him like this. He was so upset it made him look years older. Was it something to do with that news story?

"Did you know that guy?" she asked.

And he looked at her in the strangest way.

It was up to 90 degrees by noon, but Carl stayed in his office on the East side of the house where the sun came in, sweating and drinking Corona and trying to think. She was downstairs listening to Fleetwood Mac on the stereo. Occasionally she'd come up and ask him if it was okay if she called her mom and he'd have to remind her that they were out of town.

She'd forgotten about the news broadcast, of course. There'd been more on Channel 9, but it didn't tell him much. The fire department was called by a neighbor at around five-thirty a.m., but by then the whole house had already been engulfed. An architectural landmark, they said it was. A real loss. They'd been pretty sure it was arson from the first moment. When they found the cans of gasoline and discovered that someone had locked the dog in the detached garage for safety, they were ready to call it suicide.

Martin Ackerman was notified of his brother's death at around six-thirty in the morning. He found a suicide note left in his mailbox before he was taken to identify what was left of the body. The contents of the note were undisclosed. No one seemed to question why Martin Ackerman would check his mailbox at a time like that.

The grass was looking dry in the back and he couldn't remember when he'd watered it last. He walked downstairs and waved at Jesse as he passed, but she was listening to "Miracles" and didn't notice him.

He went outside, picking up the pronged metal pole he used to turn on the sprinklers.

Frank had gone to see his brother, to follow up on their one, pathetic lead, and now he was dead. He hooked the forked end of the pole around the spigot and turned it.

The sprinklers shot up and began to spit and hiss, the water forcing its way out into intersecting arcs and covering the air above the grass with rainbows.

Or had Frank's going to see Martin merely been an excuse, a way for Frank to flee from this house once he had understood how Jesse felt about Carl? Had that made him see that she was lost to him for good? Had that made him feel there was nothing worth living for?

The sprinkler next to the greenhouse and right under the birdfeeder was still spitting fitfully as if something was clogging it. He pranced through the mist to check it out. There was a heavy layer of seed husks covering the area – he brushed the sprinkler head clean and it shot up and sprayed, drenching him thoroughly.

He wiped the water from his face and started to walk back to the house. He'd only gone a couple of steps when he heard a sound coming from the greenhouse. He turned to look and was surprised to hear a loud crack, like thunder right on top of him, and to see a bright bolt of electric light flash inside his eyes.

Then he was on his knees in the wet grass, about to topple over. He caught himself and saw a two by four, the kind that kept the shelves propped up in the greenhouse, fall to the ground next to him. Somebody had just hit him on the bead with that, and he laughed a little when he realized that he'd actually seen stars, just like they do in the cartoons.

Fingers crossed the back of his head and forced him to the ground, shoving his face into the sprinkler so that the water blinded him. He twisted to one side and saw the two by four swinging back up in the air. He screwed his eyes shut and tried to cover himself, but the board came back to his head and the thunder and lightning came back and the echo took a long time to die away.

He pulled his face from the muddy grass and tried to stand. He'd barely lifted his head when a wave of pain hit him so hard that he thought the two by four had come back. But it was lying safely beside him. He twisted his head around and saw no one there. He was very happy that he wasn't going to be hit anymore.

He's gone for Jesse, Carl thought. He took a swallow of water from the sprinkler beneath him and thanked God he hadn't been knocked unconscious; he could still get there in time. He pushed himself up to his hands and knees, but his palms slipped on the wet grass and he thudded to the ground, his head feeling as if it had been hit again, this time by all the two by fours in the world.

He pushed himself up again and started crawling through the water toward the house, straining to hear anything through the hissing of the sprinklers. The record was still playing. Was that good or bad? Why couldn't he move faster? Because he was so damned tired, he told himself. True, he hadn't been knocked unconscious and thank God for it, but a nap sure would feel good right now, he thought, as his face fell forward into the cool wet grass and his eyes rolled shut.

THIRTY-TWO

Carl left a trail of water behind him as he ran from room to room, new starbursts filling his head each time his feet slapped on the floor. All he could find were notes telling her not to leave and that he'd be back soon.

———

Martin Ackerman's eyes were red and swollen as he carried another load of trash from his garage down to the corner. Only three more boxes and it would be all gone, hauled to some landfill somewhere. Let the sea gulls and rats peck and claw at it to get the food underneath. Then it would only live in his memory. Perhaps he could forget it too, but he doubted that. Forgetting came easier to some than to others.

He walked up the driveway; he'd never noticed before how steep it was, it took all his strength to walk it. Three more boxes to go, he thought as he climbed. Then the past would be gone. There ought to be a way to cut into the brain, he thought, substitute other's memories for your own. Happy ones that didn't have to do with death and killing and suicide.

He was almost to the garage before the wet hands fell on him and shoved him into the darkness. He stumbled into the garage and twisted around to see a figure, silhouetted against the bright sunlight, pulling the cord on the automatic door to close it. He ran to the kitchen door, but the man was there first.

"Where is she?" the man asked.

Martin thought he knew the voice, but he couldn't place it. He tried dodging behind the man, but he grabbed him and shoved him again, knocking him against the three boxes. Martin fell to the floor in a cascade of papers and photograph albums – the trash he'd been trying to unload. Letters were clinging to the man's wet clothes as he picked Martin up by the collar and dragged him out of the debris.

"Where is she?" he asked again. "Tell me or I'll kill you, I swear I will."

Martin fell limp in his hands.

The man let Martin fall to the floor again, crossed to the door and switched on the light and then Martin recognized Carl.

"Where is she?"

Carl's eyes were wild. His hair was matted with blood and there was a comically large bump on the back of his head.

"Don't you think I'll kill you?" he went on.

Martin didn't answer.

"Tell me where Jesse is."

Martin blinked at him, looking foolish there, with papers from the boxes still crumpled underneath him where he'd been dragged. "Jesse's dead."

"You better hope that's not true." Carl crossed to the workshop table and picked up a hammer. "Where is she?" he asked.

"She's dead." His voice was quiet and without emotion and he wasn't even trying to get up. "I thought you saw it all. Or your friend did. That's right, you had a friend. He saw her jumping in and saw us watching her. Watching the waves take her further and further away until we couldn't see her anymore. So she's gone. They're all gone. Jeff and Jesse. Now Frank, too. I'm the only one who remembers."

"What happened to Jeff?" Carl said, stepping forward, hammer in his hand.

"Nothing, he's fine."

"You just said he was gone."

"I was mistaken."

Carl squatted next to him and grabbed his wrist and held up the hammer. "I'll break your hand."

"Why?" He seemed only mildly curious.

"What happened to Frank?"

"Did you know him?"

"Yes."

"I don't understand you."

"What did you do to him?"

"My brother was never strong. I don't think what I did was wrong, not in itself. But it was more than he could take, I should have seen that."

"What was more than he could take?"

"Watching her die. We'd all been doing that for months, but now...now there was no choice. No way out for her at all. So I just let her swim away. But he was there. I should have let him go in after her, because he was dead from then on. Last night was just a formality."

"So that made it okay to kill him?"

"To do what?"

"Where is she?"

He wiped his eyes and focused on Carl for the first time. "Are you all right? What's that blood by your ear?"

"You hit me with a two by four."

"A concussion can be very serious."

He shoved Martin back with the head of the hammer. "Where is she?"

"She's dead."

"You know that's a lie."

"What are you talking about?"

"She didn't drown. She made it to shore. She made it to me and I'm not going to let you hurt her again."

"A concussion can do very serious things."

"Frank came here last night to get that letter and you killed him."

"What letter?"

"The one you said was from Jeff. It was a lie, wasn't it?"

"I understand. You never got to make peace with her. And it's too late now. Frank felt the same way."

Carl turned away and walked to the paint spattered sink. He turned the spigot, cupped his hands full of cold water and splashed it on his face. The pain in his head was only just leaving and he still felt dizzy sometimes. He'd scraped the side of his car on a guardrail on the way over because the world had seemed to split in two on him.

He applied a little water to the sticky matted hair on the back of his head and turned back to Martin. He hadn't moved. Carl rummaged through the scattered papers on the oil stained floor. They were letters mostly. From Jesse and Frank. Notes dating back to grade school between the two brothers. Love letters from Jesse to Martin. One or two from Jesse to Frank. The souvenirs of a lifetime. Martin looked at him as he glanced through them, but didn't say anything. He'd been throwing his whole past away.

Carl picked up a picture of Frank and Jesse and Martin all in front of Frank's cabin in the desert. Happier days, he thought, slipping it into his pocket. The letters from Jeff were in a separate bundle. He found the one he'd been looking for and read it again and again under the naked bulb. Martin just stared at him.

Carl had read it five times. "There's no date on this," he said to Martin. "He doesn't name the month or the season. He could have written this any time. Your maid's from Peru, isn't she? She could have jut sent it to her people and had them send it back here, so it would be postmarked after Jesse died. He never left here did he?"

Martin glanced down to the floor like a guilty schoolboy. Carl rushed to him and lifted him up by the armpits, shoving him against the wall. The blood pulsed in Carl's head, the pain almost blinding him. "That's right, isn't it?"

"Pretty much."

"Where is Jeff?"

The pain ebbed and he watched Martin's eyes; they were too dead to bother lying. "Jeff is fine."

He let Martin go and he slumped onto the floor again. Carl crouched down there with him. "Do you know where she is, Martin?" He wasn't demanding anymore. "Do you know if she's okay?"

"I'm sorry. I didn't know you still loved her. You'd think if so many people loved you, you wouldn't die so fucking alone."

Carl looked at the wrecked man, lying amidst the crumpled papers. "Do you really believe she's dead?"

"I saw her drown. I thought that would be the end of it." He eyed Carl, curious. "You think I hurt Frank? Why would I do that? He was my brother."

"He was your wife's lover."

Martin laughed, just once. "Oh, that..." He got up on his knees and started rooting through the piles of letters that surrounded him.

"What are you doing?" Carl asked.

Martin pulled one of the letters out and handed it to Carl. "I know you won't believe me. Let Jesse tell you."

Carl looked at the letter, recognizing Jesse's handwriting. He retreated to the light to read it. While he read, Martin talked on, knowing he was being ignored. "I loved her too. No one seems to believe that. Okay, I didn't talk about it. I didn't suffer the way you and Frank did. Maybe I didn't feel it as deeply. But just because I'm shallow, that doesn't mean I can't love."

Carl lowered the letter and looked at Martin. What little blood had been in Carl's face was gone now and he was white as a ghost. He asked Martin a few questions, his voice trembling. Martin answered them as best he could, not wanting to blacken his brother's memory too deeply.

Then Carl swung open the garage door and walked back to his car in the dazzling sunlight. He took the two letters with him.

Just as well; two less to throw away. When he was gone. Martin gathered up the letters and pictures and put them back in the boxes for the trash men to collect.

———◆———

Carl had forgotten to turn off the sprinklers. They were still going when he got home, drenching the two-by-four as it glistened among the heavy blades of grass. He remembered it falling next to him, then rising to strike him again.

He remembered what he'd heard on the all-news station on the way home. A teen-ager had tried to kill herself this morning by tying a plastic bag around her head. She was in the hospital now in a coma. The day before she'd accused a teacher of molesting her; she had not been believed. The school board was investigating the way the principal had handled the situation. The police had tried to interview the accused teacher, but he had apparently gone into hiding. An APB was posted for him now. His name was Ted Ryan.

Carl remembered him. He remembered a lot of things. So he knew where he had to go now.

THIRTY-THREE

There were four of them on the boat when it pulled out of the Marina and headed into open ocean. It was a homey gathering; a brother and a sister and two brothers going for a pleasure cruise. Jeff had only been back for a day and a half, but already it felt like an eternity.

Jeff never saw the ocean except when he was in the North. He knew that the ocean was in Peru too, but the notion of going to the beach was, of course, an impossibility and even now it seemed a luxury that was almost sinful.

Jessica would have laughed at him for that. She would have told him to stop acting so superior, that being a lawyer was nothing to be ashamed of. Then Jeff would ask what Martin charged and how he helped those who couldn't pay; the U.S. legal system would come into question and things would get ugly.

But that was how it would have been. Now there was only silence and quiet politeness and no one else to take his mind off the obscenity of Los Angeles.

Father Tim had tried to dissuade him from coming home this time. Jeff knew he was afraid he wouldn't come back. Jeff always struck people as soft and even after a year of proving himself, there was still suspicion that a glimpse of the good life would be enough to turn him off the track. They couldn't have been more wrong. Nothing here seemed like home.

L.A. was a sprawling, decaying mess, uglier by far than the most wretched village he'd ministered to. Of course, Jesse would have laughed at that statement too, and called him a reverse snob.

But she was not there to argue with him now. She was sitting on the deck, staring at the sky in silence, while he huddled with Martin and Frank and watched her. No, Frank watched her. Martin drove (he was sure that wasn't the right word) the boat with perfect concentration.

"It's one of the few places where she's at peace," Frank said. "I suppose there's something neutral about it. She used to sail when she was young."

"I know that," Jeff said.

More silence. The wake behind them was funnel shaped, like the tail of a fish.

People even suffered differently here. They get strange diseases of the soul that leave them untouched physically but empty out their interiors, like a child hollowing a Jack-o'-Lantern.

Jessica did not know who he was. Martin had been vague and typically clinical in his letter. Frank had been secretive and typically apologetic in his phone call. Nothing they had said had prepared him for the idea that she wouldn't know him. Frank and Martin were disappointed too. They had hoped for something from this reunion, what he wasn't sure. A shock, perhaps, that would bring it all back.

Instead there was nothing, only a glimmer of fear because she did see something familiar in the face, but transformed in a way that unnerved her. Martin and Frank were simply strangers, no more, no less. But his face that claimed to be her brother's and had enough of his shadow that it seemed like he had swallowed Jeff up, this was frightening. He was like a premonition to her, a frightening vision of the future. She locked herself in a room and didn't come out till she forgot about the incident. That took about fifteen minutes.

After that Martin insisted that they keep Jeff's identity from her; it was too disturbing. So she accepted him as another stranger, only looking at him oddly now and then as if something was about to come to her. It didn't.

Martin turned off the motor and the boat began to drift on the placid blue water. There was one other boat, a dirty fishing trowel (another wrong word, he was sure) on the horizon. He belched again, finding it a necessary way to keep his stomach in check. Martin pulled out a large knife and began to whittle on a bit of white wood. An oddly down home exercise, Jeff thought.

"Are you making something?" he asked.

Martin looked up at him in surprise. "I suppose I should think of something. My doctor recommended I take up a hobby for my blood pressure."

Typical, thought Jeff. Those with no problems must find them to use the worry parts of their brains. But wasn't it cruel of Jeff to say this man had no problems? Where was Jessica to chastise him?

Jessica was sitting over there, looking at the fishing scow (that sounded better). Frank said she was the same girl he'd always known; she'd just lost the years between then and now. Martin said it was because of something growing in her brain. He said that after it took her soul (but those weren't his words) there would be nothing to do but make her peaceful.

But there was nothing ill about his sister; she looked as healthy as he had ever seen her, even if a bit overweight. She was simply emptying her mind of dross, Jeff thought. How much was there really worth remembering, after all?

They said she thought she was seventeen and he remembered her then. She didn't look too much different to him. One's older siblings are always the same age; older. She had her first boyfriend then, Carl, and he loved to play with Jeff. They would all go together to the movies. He saw <u>Star Wars</u> with Carl. They had ice cream. He had been sorry when Carl broke up with his sister and had never liked any of her other boyfriends.

Seventeen had been a good age for Jessica and it didn't surprise him that she should retreat there, now that her brain was being eaten. After high school she had seemed to wander, never finding a use for her intelligence and her emotions. She drifted from relationship to relationship. He half suspected her of getting an abortion, but he thrust the idea from his mind as being too horrible to consider.

If he had been able to convert her, he felt sure her life would have been very different. But she'd been too threatened by his own calling for him to even speak of it to her. It had been jealousy, he supposed. She'd been more parent to him than his mother and father, so when he accepted The Church it had seemed like a rejection of her. The way she'd acted, he might have been joining some cult, indeed that was exactly how she thought of Catholicism, despite being half-heartedly raised in it herself. And when he had embraced liberation theology, which even he recognized as fanaticism, she was sure he'd gone mad. She'd been able to picture him as a nice Bing Crosby priest in the suburbs somewhere, but going down to Peru and working with Communists was more than she could bear.

But she bore it. She teased him, but she never cut him off. She didn't understand him, but she was still his sister and that would never change. Even now it hadn't changed, and if he could just go back to being the brother she recognized, she'd take care of him as always. That was of course what she had always wanted, even before the disease, for him not to grow up. So even the thing in her brain hadn't changed things, just made them more concrete.

The aimlessness of her life was his greatest pain. In a way it hurt him far more than the starvation and maiming he'd witnessed in the South. Partly that was because she was his family, but that wasn't everything. It was the waste that hurt. The people in Ayacucho had no chances. To grow up and old without losing a loved one, without being crippled in your heart or body was an impossibility. Jessica had every possibility, every advantage. Food on the table and a safe house and a promise of that forever. Now she sat there, looking at the waves, living only in weird quarter hour fragments. Martin and Frank were heartbroken at this change, but to Jeff it seemed only an intensification of her normal condition. She had always sat there and only hoped each moment would be pleasant. He didn't think there was anything growing in her brain. It was just the nothingness of her life taking over. And it was the same with all of them, Jeff thought, looking at Martin and Frank. Jessica was just the only one honest enough to die from it.

If she could have found the Lord, if he could have helped her to that, then he would have made a difference on this earth, a difference that mattered to him more than the gushing arteries he'd stopped and the crying children he'd comforted. They had suffered more, but they were strangers to him. In his own home he'd failed.

Of course, it wasn't too late. He could convert her now. And then she'd forget it all in five minutes and he'd have to do it all over again and again. It might be a worthwhile way to spend a life.

Martin stood up and walked into the sunlight, stretching himself and flexing his fingers around the knife.

"Will you be going back?" Frank asked him.

"I don't know," he said.

Frank maneuvered a cigarette into his mouth and lit it, gracefully with his one hand. Jeff remembered the first time he had seen a severed limb. A nine-year-old girl had had her family slaughtered by the Shining Path terrorists, but in a rare moment of mercy they had only raped her and cut off her arm. Since then he had seen more mangled limbs than he could remember. He doubted that Frank had lost his so dramatically.

Jeff got up and walked over to his sister. She looked up at him in some surprise, shading her eyes with her hand. A silver necklace glinted around her neck – a little pendant with her name and address on it, like a dog's I.D. tag. If found lost of wandering, please return to owner, he thought, bitterly.

"Hi," she said, with a friendly smile.

"I'm your brother Jeff," he said.

She stared at him, squinting into the sun.

"That's right, I'm all grown up. This is like those Twilight Zone episodes we used to sneak downstairs and watch in the middle of the night. A flash forward. You're getting to see the future."

She just kept looking at him, squinting into the sun.

"I'm going to be a priest. Maybe. I'm living in Peru, helping people. I think you'd be proud of me."

She was glancing away from him now, looking for a way out. He was losing her.

"You married a rich, handsome lawyer. You're very happy. Everything turns out fine."

She stood up and walked to the cabin. Martin and Frank were staring at Jeff, accusing him with their eyes. He'd committed the worst sin; he'd upset her.

She was looking from face to face, trying to find a point of reference. Martin stepped forward, calming and reassuring.

"What's the matter, Jesse? Don't you recognize us? We're your parents' friends, I'm Martin and this is my brother Frank. This is our friend..."

The idea of this structure Martin was creating to let her live out her last days in tranquility and ignorance finally repulsed him. "I'm Jeff, Jesse, I'm your brother."

Martin tried to push him aside, angrily, but he slipped by him and moved nearer to Jessica, who stared at him in wonder and almost knew him.

"They say you're sick. That there's something wrong with your brain, but I don't believe it, I think you're just dead inside and you need to wake up. You need to feel what's going on!"

She backed away but he kept moving towards her.

"You know that it's me, Jesse, I can see it, you recognize me. Let me help you. You can't just throw it all away, you can't hide from it, that won't work."

She was whispering at him now, "You're crazy, you're fucking crazy."

Martin tried to pull him back to the cabin, but he shook him off and kept at her. "You know I'm not crazy. I'm Jeff. Do I have to prove it to you? We used to cut school when Mom was working and break into our house and spend the day watching TV, I caught you with your shirt off with Carl in your room once and you made me swear never to tell…"

"Jeff," she whispered. "What have you done with Jeff? Where is he?"

She was on him, then, scratching at him and slapping him. He tried to grab her hands and stop her and make her think.

"I'm Jeff, I'm your brother and I love you. I want to help you, I want to let God help you. Jesse, listen to me!"

But now Martin was there too, trying to restrain her and then all Jeff saw of the world was a flurry of arms and hands. He was trying to tell Jessica about how God was the only one who could help her and Martin was telling him to shut the fuck up and Jesse just kept asking what they'd done with Jeff.

"If you've hurt him, I'll kill you," she said.

Somehow she had the whittling knife in her hand and she slashed out with it, cutting at Jeff's throat. It didn't hurt, but from the way the blood started pumping out of it, he knew it was an artery, though he couldn't remember its name. He'd seen this wound before and he knew where to put the pressure to stop the bleeding, but it was hard to find the spot on his own throat, especially when it was glistening with hot blood. It didn't take long, he knew, seconds and his veins would be empty. But his fingers kept working the wound and he just couldn't find the damned spot and all he could hear was his sister screaming his name.

THIRTY-FOUR

The cold desert wind was already beginning to cut at Frank as he struggled with the shovel to refill the shallow hole. The coyotes would find it, he supposed. Let them have it. It'll do some good that way. His own arm had been thrown into a landfill somewhere, he supposed. Better to feed the coyotes than rats.

He turned to walk back to the cabin, dropping behind a stunted shrub when car lights washed by from the highway. They disappeared; someone driving to somewhere, paying no attention to him. But he had to be safe. Tomorrow they'd be across the border and they'd keep driving till they reached a place where no one knew they were both dead.

He stood up and walked on, the landscape cold and blue under a huge half moon. As he moved he saw it all again in his mind, the way he did so often. Jeff, hysterical, was chanting some inane religious diatribe at her. Jessica struggling, lashing out at him with the knife. Her screaming at him, screaming Jeff's name while his blood pulsed out at her. He'd never known if she'd recognized him then, if in his pain the face of the boy had come back, or if she was calling for his help. He hoped she hadn't known, but either way it hardly mattered.

Frank had grabbed for her, trying to comfort her, but they were all attackers to her then, and the horror of what she'd done, even if she'd thought Jeff was a stranger, was too much. She broke from him and jumped into the water. He'd tried to go after her, but Martin held him back. It was better this way, he said. There was really no hope for her now. There'd be a hearing, a trial perhaps. She'd be taken away. Put in a home where no one cared for her. And even if the miracle happened and she was cured, how could she ever live with what she had done?

They watched her swim away from them in terror. The fishing boat they'd seen before was gone. There was nothing but empty water to swim to, but to her that still seemed safer than staying with them.

Frank had fallen to the deck, clinging to Martin's leg, crying, not able to watch her die. When she was out of sight they washed Jeff's blood off the deck and dropped his body into the sea, resolving to tell no one what she had done. They must protect her memory, Martin had said, and he hadn't even meant it as a joke.

Carl crouched below the window and looked around the corner of the cabin. Frank was still out there, looking at the moon. It would be better if he was further away, but there might not be another time. He pulled his sweater off, wrapped it around a rock and smashed out a windowpane. He picked out the jagged glass, reached in and opened the French doors. He ran through the bungalow, throwing open doors till he found one that was locked.

"Who's there?" she said from inside.

Carl leaned against the door in relief, breathing heavily, watching for Frank to come bursting in on him.

"It's Carl."

"Oh thank God, I know this sounds crazy but I don't know where the hell I am."

He didn't answer. He didn't trust his ability to kick open the solid oak door, so he looked around for the key, praying that it wasn't in Frank's pocket. He spotted one on an end table by the front door – an old skeleton key, black with age.

He grabbed it, clumsily, and rushed to slip it in the lock, terrified that he'd break it. It rolled over with a loud clank and he pulled open the door. She was on him in a second, kissing him. She had another white dress on. Frank must be partial to the style.

"Carl, I have to tell you something," she said.

"We have to get out of here," He tried to pull her arms off him.

"I think I'm pregnant."

"I know and it's okay. We're going to get through this together." He turned her toward the French doors, but stopped when he heard her gasp.

Frank was in the living room, leaning on a sand caked shovel.

"Hi, Carl," he said.

Jesse tried to pull away. Carl held on to her. "It's okay," he said, "this is a friend of mine."

Frank sat down, limply, at the old mission library table in the corner, chin in his hand, looking at Carl in weary irritation. "How the hell did you know?"

"When you hit me, you shoved me into the sprinkler, so I wouldn't see your face. So you had to be someone I knew. And you had to drop the board before you grabbed me and then pick it up again. If you'd had two arms you wouldn't have had to do that. Also, when you saw her at my house you knew she'd changed her clothes, even though I never told you what she'd been wearing. I have to admit, that didn't occur to me till just now."

"But didn't you think I was dead?"

"Well, that stumped me for awhile, but then I thought…well, love finds a way. That was Ryan's body, wasn't it?"

"Yeah…" he frowned and rubbed his eyes with the heel of his hand. "I really thought that would work. You haven't told anyone about this have you?"

Carl didn't answer, and Frank smiled. He turned his eyes to Jesse.

"You see, I figured if people thought we were both dead, we could really go our own way. But it always came down to getting a decoy body, and how the hell did you do that? I couldn't see killing someone just for the sake of my happiness. Then I met Ryan and well...I'd've killed him for no reason at all."

Jesse knew enough to be frightened. She held onto Carl's arm. "What's he talking about?"

Frank smiled at her. "Oh, don't ask him. He hasn't understood what was going on from the beginning." He started playing with the drawer on the desk in front of him, absently opening and shutting it. "Martin didn't try to kill anyone. I made that up...or you did, I can't remember which. She tried to kill herself – I'm sorry Jesse, but I have to tell him this, I owe him that. Afterwards...I couldn't function. I couldn't see how I could live through the next day, the first day without her. I just sat in the living room of her house, staring at the door, praying for her to walk in. And she did."

"Martin was gone, I should say, doing something responsible with the police or the Coast Guard or something. He felt it was important to keep busy. I didn't. I didn't feel much of anything."

"So there was a knock on the door, as I said, and it was Jesse. I thought I'd gone mad, but it was really her. There was a terrified woman with her, a Mexican, I think. They'd picked her up in front of the fishing boat and from the blood all over her, they'd known something was wrong. They were illegal and they were afraid to get mixed up with the authorities so her man wanted to just drop her off on shore, but the woman felt sorry for her. She talked him into letting her stay that night. In the morning she tried to take her home, but the place she said she lived wasn't there anymore."

"The woman started to get more and more scared till she saw the necklace around Jesse's throat with an address on it and brought her home. She said she hoped she hadn't done wrong and then she ran off."

"Jesse didn't know where she was, of course, or who I was. But I had her there, and no one else knew it. She'd come back to me, whether she meant to or not, and I wasn't about to let her go."

"Martin was already a widower, by his own choice, so he had no claim on her. Whose was she, if not mine? So I took her home."

Frank was staring at the desktop as he spoke. Carl tried to move Jesse to the door, very slowly, trying not to make Frank look up. He didn't look up – he just took an old revolver from the desk drawer and set it on the table in front of him. Carl stopped.

Frank looked up at Jesse, spinning the gun like a top on the old wood table. "We'd talked about it many times before, of course, you and I going off together. Now I finally had the courage to do it."

"I kept you for a month and you never knew who I was. Sometimes you believed me when I told you your parents had left you with me. When I went out, I had to lock you in, but I hated to do that, so I didn't go out much. I stayed with you nearly all the time. We didn't talk much, because we had nothing to talk about. We could listen to music, but we couldn't watch movies like we used to because you always forgot the story. Still, we were together. Like we always wanted to be. And in all that time, you never trusted me. You never trusted me for a moment."

"Then one time I had to go out and when I came back you had run away, you had…escaped from me. I wondered if I hadn't dreamed the whole thing. Then Carl came along and I knew I'd get you back. You'd come back to me once before, and now you came back to me again. So it's obvious that, despite the relative hardships we've gone through, we are meant to be together. And I find that comforting."

Jesse's fingers were digging into Carl's arm as she listened. Carl was doing his best to move toward the desk without moving at all. "Why did Ryan's body have only one arm?"

"Oh, I cut it off."

Jesse gasped. Frank looked stricken and hurried to set things right. "I know it sounds grotesque, but I did it for you. And like most things that sound horrible, once you're actually doing it... well, it just becomes part of life. I left the suicide note at my brother's house first. Then I went to see Ryan...to apologize. I let him charm me for a while, I knew that would relax him. Then I took this out," Frank picked up the gun and held it, for the first time, like a weapon. "I brought him out to my car. I made him drink a Coke with some Halcion in it and by the time we were in my garage he was sleeping like a baby."

"I had to do it without leaving any marks, and I didn't want to hurt him. I didn't want to be cruel. So I took a hose and ran it from the exhaust pipe in through the window and left the motor going for an hour or so. I have no idea if it takes that long to kill someone, but I figured, better safe than sorry. After I made sure he was dead, I wrapped his arm in a garbage bag, used a hacksaw, and you'd be surprised how easy it came off. Then I doused everything in gasoline, set fire to it and left."

"I knew there wouldn't be enough left to identify, but the missing arm would do it."

"What about the teeth?" Carl asked.

Frank looked at him, surprised.

"That's how they identify burn victims," Carl explained, "Dental records. Or DNA."

Frank shrugged. "Only if they're suspicious."

"Suicide? Arson? Don't they have to investigate?"

"That costs money. Martin's already identified me."

"Has he?"

"It's in the papers."

"Maybe."

"Don't play tricks with me."

"Be a shame if you killed him for no reason."

"There was a reason. He raped her."

"And you couldn't."

Frank blinked.

Carl went on, unblinking. "I know all about it. You never had an affair with her."

Frank laughed, a beat or so too late. "What are you talking about?"

"I know what happened here. On your idyllic weekend. The one you'll never forget."

Frank sat upright, looking stern. "Martin's been telling you stories. He doesn't know. I'm the only guy who knows and I told you."

"I didn't get it from Martin. I got it from Jesse."

He glanced at her, confused, vulnerable.

"She wrote him a letter," Carl pulled it from his jeans. "Told him the whole story. How you tried to seduce her up here. How she tried to turn you down, gently, and you tried to force yourself on her. Only you couldn't get it up, so you just wound up lying on the floor, crying, like a little boy, she said. Sobbing into the little piece of white dress you'd ripped off her."

Frank's eyes shot from Carl to Jesse, looking for some confirmation or denial. All she gave him was fear. "She never wrote to Martin. Martin didn't know, he never said anything."

"They didn't want to hurt your feelings." He unfolded the letter and began to read.

"*God, I don't know what to do. Part of me wants to call the police, but another part feels like such a bitch for even telling you about this. I don't think he would ever have really hurt me, but at the same time I was there and I know what he tried to do. And God, the way he cried and apologized all the way home. Three hours never felt so long. And then when I got him home and pulled into his driveway to drop him off, he actually tried to kiss me, like we'd been on a date or something. I know what he's been through, I certainly don't want him to have another breakdown, but how can I deal with this? He's your brother. He's my friend, when I think about all the time I spent helping him fix up his house and his*" *garden, trusting him, liking him. And I still like him. I just want to pretend this never happened. But will he let me do that? Can I do that?"*

Carl raised his eyes from the letter. "So that's your affair. That's the story of your life."

Frank was still looking at Jesse. "Don't listen to this," he said to her.

"When she got sick," Carl went, "you started telling people you'd had an affair with her. And since nobody particularly liked Martin, they were ready to believe you. The more you told people and the more they told other people, the more real the story became. It was almost as good as having the affair for real, and a lot less trouble. It gave a poetry to your whole life. And it successfully erased this embarrassing scene," Carl gestured to the letter. "And even if you do create a memory out of thin air, if you believe it enough to really remember it, who's to say it didn't happen?"

Frank's face lighted with sudden inspiration. "That letter's a lie. It was an excuse she came up with when she thought he found out about us."

"I don't think so. Tell me, when you had her hidden in your house for a month, were you able to get it up then?"

Frank was silent and his face seemed to sag with age. Then he whispered, "I never intentionally hurt her."

"But you did screw her?" Carl tried to make it sound as ugly as he could.

"I love her," was all Frank could say.

"I know you do. That's why you want to take her away from all of this, so you can spend the rest of your life raping her and feeling guilty watching her forget."

"And you haven't been fucking her?" Frank snapped back.

"No more than she wanted me to."

Frank stood up, the gun shaking slightly in his hand. "Jesse, move away from him."

She clung to Carl tighter.

"What are you going to do with her?" Carl asked.

"Take care of her. Live with her. That's all I've wanted. And whether the memory is false or real, that doesn't change the way I feel about her, or the way we are together."

"The way you are together is she's terrified and you're crazy. She loves me. I'm the only one she feels safe with."

Frank glanced down for a second, thinking. Then he was back. "I don't care. She's the only thing in my life. I've killed for her. I want her for myself."

"What did you do to Jeff?" Carl asked. He felt Jesse flinch.

Frank glanced at her nervously. "You were wrong about that. He's in Peru."

"Jeff," whispered Jesse.

"I don't think so. Did he find out you were hiding her? Was he the first one you killed?"

Frank smiled. "That's right, I'm a psycho killer. Now tell Jesse to move out of the way so I can kill you too."

Jesse stepped in front of Carl. "No, listen," she said, her voice quavering, "I don't understand this, but you say you love me. You must know I'll never forgive you if you hurt Carl."

"Yes, you will," Frank said.

She jumped toward Frank. Frank stumbled and Carl grabbed for the gun, feeling it jerk in his hand and heard a loud explosion. There was a hot pain in Carl's stomach. He fell back against the wall and slumped to the floor.

Frank stepped back, looking down at him. "I'm sorry." He snatched the letter out of Carl's pocket with the rubber tips of his metal hand, glancing over at Jesse reproachfully. "I can't believe you wrote Martin about us."

He shoved the letter into his pocket and turned to Jesse, who was pressing herself in a corner by the front door. "Move, we're getting in the car."

"No way," she said.

He stared at her.

"I'm not going with you," she went on. "Whatever you're gonna do, get it over with here, I'm not leaving him."

Frank glanced at Carl, twisting on the floor, holding his stomach. She wouldn't leave as long as she could see him here. He stuck the gun in his belt, grabbed Carl's arm and started dragging him from the room.

"Come on," Frank said, "out of sight, out of mind."

Carl groaned and Frank kept pulling. It was hard work because Carl kept twisting around, but Frank got him as far as the bedroom door. He flung open the door and bent over Carl again, pausing to take a breath.

Carl hauled himself up onto his elbow, grabbed the gun in Frank's belt, twisted it around and fired.

Frank staggered back, looking at Carl in surprise. A dark stain was spreading on his shirt and he touched it, wondering. Then he understood. He cursed and snatched the gun from Carl's trembling hands. He leveled it at Carl. Carl covered his face with his hands and Frank fired.

Jesse screamed when she saw the blood pumping from Carl's hands. Frank turned to her, pointing at her with the gun.

"Out," he said.

She was too afraid to resist now. She backed out the front door and Frank staggered after her.

"Get in the car," he whispered, not for fear of being heard, but because he hurt too much to speak. He fell against the side of the car, pulled open the passenger door and climbed in. Jesse was behind the wheel.

"Go," he said, "get me to a hospital."

Jesse stared at him, helplessly. "I don't have the keys."

Frank reached into his pants pocket, wincing with pain and pulled the keys free, yanking the letter out with them. The dark stained pages fluttered out across the sand. He tossed the keys into her lap. "For God's sake, Jesse, hurry."

She started the car and pulled out into the desert.

"I don't know where I'm going," she said.

"I'll tell you. Just listen to me. Just do what I tell you."

The last thing he saw as the car went down the long drive was a coyote digging at something in the sand.

"Hey?"

There was no answer.

"I'm getting a little tired of driving."

Frank's head was resting against the window.

"The last sign said sixty miles to Los Angeles."

The white line seemed to glow in the headlights.

"Hey, you."

No answer.

"How long before we get home?"

When the doorbell rang at four thirty in the morning, Mr. and Mrs. Fletcher hurried down the stairs, feeling equal parts apprehension, concern and anger.

Then they opened the front door and Mrs. Fletcher started screaming.

The woman stood on the front step like an apparition. Hair wild from the wind. Eyes burning. White dress drenched in blood.

A car was half on the driveway and half on the lawn. The door was open so the interior light was on. You could see the passenger, slumped across the seat, black with blood, missing one of his arms.

Mr. Fletcher started screaming too.

THIRTY-FIVE

"The whole situation is really something of an ethical quagmire," Dr. Hopley said, studying how the man across from him seemed to keep his right hand covered, out of self-consciousness.

"I'm aware of that," the man replied.

It wasn't self-consciousness though. When the bullet had struck Carl's hand, it had shattered bone, ripped through tendons and severed nerves. The hand was good for very little now, but it had deflected the bullet from Carl's skull so he was grateful to it for that. And he was learning to write with his left hand.

"Though there is nothing emotionally or even psychologically wrong with her, the neurological deterioration is so extensive, an institution is really the only place for her." Dr. Hopley's voice dripped with sympathy. "For an individual to attempt to care for her on his own? The strain would be too intense. It could lead to a complete breakdown."

"I'm aware of that, too." Carl said, smiling faintly. "What of the other...condition."

"Well, that's even more of a quagmire." Carl guessed that quagmire was Dr. Hopley's word of the month. "She's not legally competent to make a decision on her own, even if she understood the situation. The State can't, of course, make it for her and neither can you. So there's nothing we can do, even though having her come to term and go through labor in her condition seems, well, terribly cruel. She won't even understand what's happening to her."

"She will, as long as I'm with her," Carl said, slowly coming to his feet. "Now will you let me see her?"

Dr. Hopley sighed. "Well, you see, that's all part of the complication. We can't allow visitations from people outside the family, without permission <u>from</u> the family. And, well, in her case, there is no family to talk to."

Martin had died from an overdose of sleeping pills the day after his brother's funeral. Carl was still in critical condition at that point and had been unable to attend.

"So you see," Dr. Hopley went on, "until we are finally able to contact her brother, I'm afraid there's nothing I can do."

"I can't wait that long. No one can."

"I'm sorry."

Carl braced himself against the desk with his good hand and leaned in. "I'm the baby's father."

Dr. Hopley nodded once, then gave in.

Carl followed Dr. Hopley through the white halls of the hospital, limping with a slow shuffling step. There were still stitches in his abdomen from where they'd taken out a few feet of his lower intestines.

"What will happen to the baby?"

"Well, that's another..."

"Quagmire?"

"Yes. She's obviously not capable of caring for it herself. I suppose the state will..."

"I'll take care of the baby."

Dr. Hopley stopped before a pair of double doors. "Well, that's very noble of you, but there may be legal complications..."

"I'll take care of the baby," he said, again.

Dr. Hopley shrugged and opened the doors. They were in the common room now. People sitting about, playing games, doing puzzles, watching televisions. It looked more like a clubhouse than a snake pit.

One woman sat alone though, staring at the floor in the corner, not looking at anyone around her.

"There she is," Dr. Hopley said, "occasionally she's quite gregarious, but mostly she's withdrawn like this. She's frightened of everyone."

Carl was moving toward her now, quickening his step, calling out to her.

She looked up and her face split into a wide grin. "Carl!" she called out and ran to him. She hugged him so hard, his eyes watered with pain.

He stumbled over to a chair and sat down. She hovered over him, full of questions.

"What is this place? Where am I?" she asked.

"Don't you remember? You're visiting me, stupid," Carl said. "I'm in the hospital. I had an accident."

"Oh, my God, are you all right?"

"I'm fine," he said, staring at her worn face, "I'm fine."

She pulled up a chair and sat close to him, her hands always touching him as if she were afraid he might vanish if she let go. She seemed so much older than when he'd last seen her. Her hair was cut short, her eyes were hollow, her face was puffy and haggard. The institutional clothes hung about her loosely, but he could still see the swelling of the child in her belly.

She didn't seem aware of it now, but he knew, in time, she would break the news to him. The news that she was carrying their child. He kissed her softly on the cheek and held her.

Of course, he knew it was Frank's child. The chronology left no doubt. The baby must have been conceived during the time Frank kept her in his house, on one of those nights when the loneliness and the misery and her blank, uncomprehending stare became too much for him. When he wanted to live the love he'd created for them.

But what did that matter? Nobody but Carl knew the truth. And I'll just forget about it, Carl thought. Forgetting is easy.

ABOUT THE AUTHOR

Phoef Sutton is a novelist, playwright, TV producer and screenwriter who was born in Washington D.C., grew up in Virginia and has lived in California for longer than he can remember.

He won two Emmys and a Golden Globe for his work on the classic TV series *Cheers* and a Peabody and a GLAAD award for *Boston Legal*. He also wrote for the cult hit *Terriers*. He divides his time between writing, watching Turner Classic Movies and going to baseball games with his wife Dawn and his daughters, Skylar and Celia.

His novels include the thriller *Crush*, the horror tales *The Dead Man: Midnight Special* and *The Dead Man: Reborn*, and *Wicked Charms*, which he co-authored with Janet Evanovich. He lives in South Pasadena, California and Vinalhaven, Maine.

Made in the USA
Middletown, DE
02 February 2017